How much did horses understand, anyway?

Callie reached for the reins. Before she could pull back on them, Star came to a crisp halt. How had Star known she wanted to stop? Had she pulled on the reins without realizing it? She sighed. She didn't want to stop riding. She wanted to keep going forever.

Star lifted her head and started walking again. It was as if she had known Callie wanted to move! That was impossible, though.

Then again, maybe not. *Stop*, Callie thought, testing the horse. Star came to a sharp, clean halt. *Walk.* Star started forward once more. Callie gasped. Somehow, Star knew her thoughts.

**Look for more *Phantom Rider* books
coming soon from Scholastic!**

Ghost Horse

by
Janni Lee Simner

A GLC Book

AN
APPLE
PAPERBACK

SCHOLASTIC INC.
New York   Toronto   London   Auckland   Sydney

No part of this publication may be reproduced in whole or in part, or stored in a retrieval system, or transmitted in any form or by any means, electronic, mechanical, photocopying, recording, or otherwise, without written permission of the publisher. For information regarding permission, write to Scholastic Inc., 555 Broadway, New York, NY 10012.

ISBN 0-590-67313-0

10 9 8 7 6 5 4 3   6 7 8 9/9 0/0

Printed in the U.S.A.   40

First Scholastic printing, June 1996

For Larry, without whom I might never have discovered the Arizona desert. And with grateful acknowledgment to Michele and Bo, my riding instructors.

Chapter One

The desert shimmered with heat.

Callie stared out the car window, watching drab brown houses disappear behind her. The houses didn't have lawns, the way houses were supposed to, but rocks and spiky cacti. The trees were thin and wispy, dusted with chalky green leaves. Distant mountains towered above the low buildings, but they were ugly and gray, nothing like the tree-filled Catskills Mom and Dad had driven through when they first left Long Island. Everything was dull and faded, as if the heat had taken all the colors away.

Callie fidgeted in the sticky backseat of the car. "If this is Arizona," she announced, "I hate it."

"Oh, stop acting like such a child," her sister, Melissa, said. Melissa brushed an auburn curl off her pale face. Callie had given up on her own tangled brown hair long ago and kept it trimmed close to her neck, even though Melissa said the haircut made her look like a boy.

"I'm not—" Callie began, but her father turned around, cutting her short.

"Callie, Melissa, please don't start. Let your mother drive in peace." Dad looked tired, and stubble shadowed his chin. For four days they'd been getting up before sunrise to drive.

From behind the wheel Mom added, "At least wait until we get to the house before you make any judgments, okay?"

"How far are we from Tucson, anyway?" Callie asked. She'd seen a few tall buildings when they'd first turned off the interstate, but that was all. The buildings had quickly given way to stores and strip malls; the stores, in turn, had been replaced by one-story houses. The real city was still somewhere up ahead—wasn't it?

"This is it." In the mirror, Callie saw Mom smile. "Isn't it beautiful? So much open space, and the sky is huge."

Too huge. The cloudless sky felt strange and close, as if it would crush Callie at any moment. A hawk flew above in lazy circles.

Callie sighed. Why did Mom's computer company have to leave New York, anyway? Dad's architecture firm had only made things worse by agreeing so easily to transfer him.

"I'm hot," Callie said. She was tired of sitting in the car; even the air-conditioning didn't seem to help much. She rolled down the window. A blast of hot air rushed in. She quickly closed it again. It was only June, still spring back at home.

"Quit complaining," Melissa told her.

"I'm not complaining. I'm just hot, that's all. And tired. And sticky. Can't we turn up the AC?"

"You are too complaining," Melissa said. "Complaining Callie, that's you." Melissa laughed. "Complaining Callie—hey, that kind of has a ring to it, don't you think?"

"Shut up," Callie said.

Melissa began to whisper, "Complaining Callie, complaining Callie . . ."

Callie jabbed her with her elbow.

"Hey!" Dad whirled around again. "No hitting!" He turned to Melissa. "Are you all right?"

Melissa, who'd looked fine a moment before, gingerly rubbed her side. "I think so." Her voice quavered. "It's not Callie's fault. She's just too young to control herself." Melissa flashed a sweet, very fake smile. Callie wanted to poke her again. Even Dad looked a little bit disgusted.

"I'm only two years younger than her," Callie said sullenly. Callie was almost thirteen, after all. "Besides, Melissa started it."

Dad sighed. "Just be quiet, okay? Both of you."

Callie didn't answer, just turned and glared out the window. She heard Dad pull open the glove compartment, looking for a map. Beside her, Melissa whispered, "Complaining Callie."

Melissa kept her voice low, so Mom and Dad couldn't hear over the hum of the air conditioner. She was good at that. Mom and Dad never noticed anything Melissa did. Callie was the one their parents always got angry at. And when Callie had something important to say, her parents never really listened. Not even when that something was as important as not wanting to leave Long Island and her friends behind, not wanting to move into the dull, dusty desert. Even though she'd seen pictures, she hadn't realized just how dry and brown the city really looked.

"Complaining Callie, complaining Callie . . ." Melissa's voice turned singsong.

Callie clenched her hands into fists. She knew that if she even looked at her sister, she'd start screaming. Instead she kept staring out the window. The houses had thinned out, and many of the cacti were the tall, branched kind she'd seen in photos and cartoons. Between two houses, in an open field, some horses grazed on scrubby yellow grass.

Callie pressed her nose against the glass for a closer look. She'd never seen horses inside a city before—not that this looked much like a city. There were six of them, all different shades of brown and gray. Their necks stretched gracefully toward the dry grass. Their manes shone in the sun. If there were horses in Tucson, it might not be such a bad place after all.

"Can I take riding lessons?" Callie had always loved horses. She had a book full of pictures of them that she looked at all the time. She'd always wanted to ride.

"We looked into that once already," Mom said. "You know how outrageous the prices were."

"Maybe they're cheaper here," Callie said.

"We'll see," Mom said. "Let's get settled in first, and we'll worry about things like riding lessons in a few weeks, okay?"

Callie watched the horses disappear behind her. A little farther on she saw a sign that read SONORAN STABLES.

Finally Mom turned onto a small side street. The car jolted; Callie looked down and saw a dirt road. Mom drove to the end of the block. She pulled into a driveway, stopping in front of the garage. A cloud of dust flew up in front of the car, then slowly settled back to the ground.

Callie had seen pictures of the house, but only Mom and Dad had actually been there. They hadn't told her the street wasn't paved. No one she knew lived on a dirt road, not unless they were all the way out in the country. What kind of city was this?

The house was only one story, built of what looked like gray clay, with bright blue trim around the edges. The awning was large, stretching out from the roof and casting shadows in front of the house. Mountains towered behind the house, not so distant now, jagged against the blue sky. Callie saw similar houses across the street. On their side of the street, though, the next house wasn't until halfway up the block.

The garage was to the house's right. To the left, Callie saw a screened patio. For several hundred feet beyond the patio, brushy trees and cacti were scattered about. Callie thought of the cool oaks and deep green grass at their house on Long Island. She didn't want to live in Tucson. She wanted to stay in the car until her parents turned around and took her back home.

"It's lovely," Melissa said, but she rolled her eyes. Callie knew that Melissa hated the house and the city, too, even if she didn't say so to Mom and Dad.

Mom shut off the engine, and with it, the air conditioner. So much for staying in the car. Callie stepped outside and stood, stretching the stiffness out of her legs.

The sun hung low and large in the afternoon sky. Callie felt heat burning against her skin. There wasn't any humidity, but the air felt heavy anyway, as if she might collapse beneath its weight if she stood outside too long. Her throat was scratchy and dry.

"I'm thirsty," Callie said. Something brushed her foot; she looked down and jumped. A dull brown lizard, nearly half a foot long, scuttled away.

"It is pretty warm," Mom agreed. She reached into the car for her keys. "Here. Go get yourself a drink of water."

Callie took the keys and ran up to the house. She unlocked the door and stepped in. The air inside felt cooler, even without any air-conditioning.

The house didn't look so bad from indoors. Gray carpet covered the living room floor. Large windows and high ceilings made the room feel open and airy. So did the lack of furniture; the movers wouldn't arrive for another day or two.

To the left of the living room, Callie found the kitchen. At the far end of the kitchen was another door, leading out onto the patio. Beyond the patio, she saw the bushes and cacti, which stopped short near the backs of other houses.

Callie turned on the faucet and cupped her hands beneath it. The water was lukewarm; she drank just enough to make her throat feel better. Then she left the kitchen and walked through the rest of the house.

On the other side of the living room there was a hallway. Callie followed it. At the end of the hall a door opened onto a huge bedroom with a bathroom inside. That was probably Mom and Dad's room. There were four other doors along the hall, two on each side. One was a second bathroom, one a linen closet. The third door led to another bedroom. The room was almost as large as Mom and Dad's, with pale blue carpet and a ceiling fan. An open door in one corner revealed a walk-in closet. Through the window, Callie saw Mom and Dad close the car doors and walk toward the house. Callie heard Melissa inside the house already. Melissa opened the fourth door as she approached, then slammed it shut again. She stepped up behind Callie.

"Cool room," she said. "I want it."

"I was here first," Callie said. The room was larger and airier than Callie's room at home. She liked it.

"I need the closet." Melissa tossed her purse and a suitcase onto the floor, as if the room were already hers. "I have more clothes than you. Besides, I'm older."

"Being the oldest doesn't mean you get whatever you want," Callie said.

Just then Dad walked up behind them.

"Dad, can I have this room?" Melissa asked

the question before Callie had the chance to say anything.

"I don't see why not," Dad said. "The rooms are about the same size, after all. Nice house, isn't it? Needs some work in the yard, which is why we got such a good price."

Callie whirled to face him. "I wanted this room!"

"There's no need to yell, Callie."

"But I was here first! I didn't even get the chance to ask!"

Dad sighed, looking even more tired than before. "Calliope Fern, ever since we left New York you've been moaning about how awful you think everything is. For once, just listen to what I say, and don't argue, okay?"

"But—"

"No *buts*. Please."

Mom called Dad from the living room; Dad turned and walked away without another word. Callie glared after him. It wasn't fair. Dad was the one who wasn't listening, not her.

Melissa closed the door behind her. Callie turned and threw it open again. Melissa sat on the floor, sorting through the clothes in her suitcase.

"I hate you!"

Melissa shrugged. "So what else is new?" She continued unpacking. Callie left the room, slamming the door shut behind her.

"No slamming doors!" Dad called from the living room.

Callie sighed. She crossed the hall to the fourth door. For just a moment she hoped that her room would be even nicer than Melissa's. Then she remembered that Melissa had already looked inside; if it were better, she would have taken it instead. With a sinking feeling, Callie opened the door.

What she saw made her hate her sister even more.

The room was filled with junk—torn boxes, battered furniture, a bed with a ripped mattress. Dust covered everything. There was no carpet, just a grubby linoleum floor turned yellow with age. The air smelled of mothballs. Callie coughed. A cloud of dust flew into the air.

At the far end of the room was a low window smudged with dirt. The screen beyond the glass was rusty. Callie crossed the room to the window and peered outside—into the ugliest backyard she'd ever seen. The ground was all dirt and brown grass, with just a few trees and paddle-shaped cacti. Rusted metal fences fell apart where they stood. Halfway across the yard, a large circle of dirt was trampled flat, and nothing grew there at all.

The land stretched gently downhill for several hundred feet, then dipped more sharply into a sandy gully. The gully wound out of sight in both directions. Beyond it Callie saw more houses. Beyond the houses, the mountains stabbed at the sky.

The yard was huge; that was one reason her parents had chosen the house. Two acres, Dad had said. But why would anyone want two acres like this?

Callie ran into the living room. Mom and Dad sat against a wall, talking quietly.

"I can't live in there!"

Dad sighed. "I thought we'd already discussed this."

"I'll take care of it." Mom stood. Mascara smudged her cheek; her red hair had come loose and fell to her shoulders. She followed Callie down the hall. "I'm sure the room's not so bad," she said.

Callie stepped back into the bedroom, hoping Mom would see why she couldn't sleep there. As soon as Mom entered the room, she started coughing.

"See?" Callie said.

Mom nodded. "Mrs. Hansen was supposed to send someone to take her things away and clean up before we arrived," she said. "I'll have to call the real-estate agent in the morning. I'm sorry, Callie. I really expected the room to be cleaned out. Your father and I are planning to

11

carpet and paint once we're settled. Just give us a couple of weeks, okay?"

"But I have to sleep here tonight!" Callie cried.

"There's nothing I can do about that." Mom's voice was calm, reasonable. It made Callie even angrier. "Unless you want to share a room with Melissa for a while."

Callie shook her head; sharing a room with Melissa sounded even worse than dealing with dust and old furniture. "What am I supposed to do with all this junk?" she asked.

"Dad and I can carry the furniture out to the garage. Pile everything else in a corner." Mom walked across the room and pushed the window open. The frame creaked with a sound like fingernails on a blackboard. "There. That should help with the dust," Mom said. "What do you think?"

"I think I want to go back to New York," Callie said.

Mom ignored Callie completely. "What I think," she said, "is that it's time for dinner. How about pizza?"

"With mushrooms?" Callie asked. Melissa hated mushrooms, though she'd never admitted the fact to Mom and Dad. Melissa never admitted to anything that made her seem less than perfect.

"You've got it. I think I saw a pizza place just a few miles back; I'll drive by. Can't order in until we have a phone, after all." Mom gave Callie a quick hug. "It really isn't so bad here," Mom said. "You'll see." She smiled at Callie, then went out to the car.

Callie stayed in the room, staring at the boxes. The walls were dirty, the windowsill covered with grime. The wallpaper—yellow with blue flowers—was peeling away. Callie opened the closet door, and a cobweb blew into her face.

Callie sighed. All the pizza in the world didn't have enough mushrooms to make Melissa pay for this.

When her mother returned with the pizza, Callie still hadn't started cleaning. She didn't know where to begin. That meant it was dark by the time she got started.

She shoved the boxes into the closet, along with a battered old trunk. When she was done, more of the dingy, yellowed floor showed than ever, but at least she had enough space to move the furniture away.

Mom and Dad carried the furniture—two battered dressers, a table, and a broken chair—to the garage. Callie had to wipe the dust away herself, though; she also had to sweep the floor. By the time she finished, her clothes were covered with dirt.

The bed Callie kept for now. At least she

wouldn't have to sleep on the floor like everyone else. She dumped her sleeping bag onto the mattress. Still more dust flew into the air. The movers had better come soon, Callie thought. She wanted her own furniture back.

She wanted her own room back, her own house. Too bad the movers couldn't do anything about that.

Callie crawled into bed, but even after the long drive, she couldn't sleep. The bedsprings jabbed at her back; no matter how often she rolled over, she couldn't get comfortable. The mattress still smelled of dust. And the room was much darker than her room ever got at home.

Outside, an owl hooted. Farther away, Callie heard a wilder, deeper sound, somewhere between yipping and howling. She shivered. Back home, the only animals she heard at night were raccoons, usually when they were knocking over garbage cans.

Her window was still open. There was a screen, so of course the animals couldn't get in—but even so, she rose to close it.

An electric tingle ran down Callie's spine, so sudden she froze in her tracks. In only a moment it was gone. She rubbed a hand against the back of her neck, then continued toward the window.

A full moon cast silver-blue light on the yard, bright enough that Callie could still see the mountains, dark shadows against the sky. The old fences, the scrubby grass, the trees and cacti all stood out clearly, though their drab colors were even less distinct than by day.

Callie hadn't known the moon had that much light. At home, the streetlights were so bright that the moon was just a pale glow in the sky, hidden by haze more often than not. The yard didn't look nearly as bad by moonlight.

There was something strange about the light, something that kept Callie staring at the empty yard. She squinted, feeling as if she were missing something, as if the yard were out of focus. The moonlight sharpened, turning so bright it hurt Callie's eyes. Within that light, she saw something.

At first she thought she imagined it. It shimmered, no more than a glowing shadow. Then all of a sudden it turned sharp and real, more real than anything else in the yard.

It was a horse. A beautiful silver horse, with a coat that glistened in the moonlight and a white mark like a star on her forehead. The star shone with a light all its own, brighter than the moon, brighter than the lights of the distant houses. The horses Callie had seen by the side of the road were dull in comparison. Callie ached to step outside, to press her cheek against the horse's sleek side, to run her hands through the soft silver mane. She opened the window wider.

She didn't know where the horse had come from, and she didn't care. She was glad it had stopped in her yard. If she had to live somewhere with wild animals, at least there were horses, too.

The horse began to move, graceful as silk, until she stood just feet away from the window. Callie stared through the screen into black, bottomless eyes. She felt suddenly calm, as if she could deal with living in a strange place after all.

She didn't know how long she watched. At some point she knelt by the window, though her gaze never left the horse. Eventually she fell asleep.

When she woke, the horse was gone.

Chapter Two

Someone screamed.

For a moment Callie was too tired to care. Her knees ached from kneeling at the window, though at some point in the night she'd rolled over onto the floor. She quickly sat up. Sweat made her pajamas cling to her skin, even though it was early morning. She looked blearily out the window. The horse was gone, the yard as ugly as ever. She saw Mom and Dad at the far end of the property, talking together.

Had the horse really been out there at all? Or had she only dreamed it?

Another scream, and Callie recognized her sister's voice. She jumped to her feet, suddenly awake after all. She ran across the hall, throwing Melissa's door open to see what was wrong.

Melissa sat on the floor, backed up against the wall; she wore a nightshirt that barely covered her knees. A huge brown bug with crablike pincers, eight legs, and a pointy tail was slowly crawling up her leg.

"Get it off me!" Melissa screamed.

"It's just a bug," Callie said.

"Don't you know anything?" Melissa said. "It's a scorpion. They're deadly!"

Panic caught at the back of Callie's throat. Why would Mom and Dad let them live somewhere with killer bugs? She looked wildly about. An open bag full of Melissa's shoes lay in one corner; Callie grabbed one. She swung it at Melissa's leg, brushing the bug to the floor. The scorpion began to skitter away; Callie slammed the shoe down on it, hard. When she pulled the shoe away, the scorpion was dead. Callie knelt beside it for a closer look. Even half smushed, it was a strange-looking bug.

Melissa's lower lip began to tremble. "It could have killed me," she whispered. Without warning, she began to cry loud, choking sobs.

The front door slammed open; a moment later Dad ran into the room. He saw Melissa crying and rushed to her side.

"Melissa, what's wrong?" He pulled Melissa into his arms. "What is it?"

Through her sobs, Melissa told him about the scorpion. "It was right on my leg," she whimpered.

"Scorpions aren't really deadly," Dad reassured her. "Though I'm told their sting does hurt a lot."

"I killed it," Callie said proudly. She pointed

to where the smushed scorpion still lay on the carpet.

Dad looked at it. "Thank you, Callie," he said. "I'm sure your sister is grateful."

Melissa shuddered. "It's gross," she said. She pulled herself more tightly against the wall. "Get it out of my room."

Anger made Callie's cheeks hot. Didn't Melissa even appreciate what she'd done? Callie jumped to her feet. "You could at least thank me!" she yelled, glaring at Melissa.

"Callie," Dad said, "your sister's just had a bit of a scare. There's no need to shout."

"You don't understand!" Callie said, yelling at Dad now, too. "Even when I'm nice to her, she doesn't care. I should have let the scorpion sting her."

"Callie!" Dad looked at her. "Don't say that."

"It's no worse than the stuff Melissa says to me. You just never hear her." Callie turned and stormed out of the room, flinging the door shut behind her.

"No slamming doors!" Dad called as Callie ran away.

If she were at home, Callie would have run to her room, collapsed onto her bed, and cried until she wasn't angry anymore. But this wasn't home, and she didn't want to spend any more time in her awful new room than she had to. She went into it only long enough to get dressed; then she ran outside.

The hot air hit her at once. She felt as though she'd stepped into an oven. Callie scowled. It was too early in the morning to be so hot.

She thought about the horse again. In the heat of day, she had trouble believing it had been anything more than a dream. She wished she could go back to sleep and dream about it again.

Callie felt heat burning through the bottoms of her sneakers. Even the ground was hot. She walked over to the car, sat down on the rear bumper, and leaned back.

The metal was burning hot. Callie yelped and jumped to her feet.

Someone giggled.

Callie looked up. Across the dirt road, a tall, lanky girl stood in front of a small, brown house, one of several that lined that side of the street. A wide-brimmed straw hat shielded the girl's eyes from the sun; limp black hair fell to her shoulders. In one hand she had a paperback book, held open with one finger. When she saw Callie watching her, she turned away and started back inside.

"Wait!" Callie ran across the street. If there was a girl her age in the neighborhood, she wanted to meet her. "What's your name?"

The girl turned back around. She squinted

down at Callie. "I'm Amy," she said. "I didn't mean to laugh at you."

"I'm Callie."

Amy brushed a hand across her face. "You're from out East, right?"

Callie blinked; she'd always thought of Arizona as out West, not New York as out East. "Yeah," she said. "How can you tell?"

"Your accent, of course."

"What accent?" If anything, Amy had the accent, speaking more slowly and softly than Callie was used to.

"You talk kind of loud and fast. Blurring your words together." Amy shrugged. "Easterners do that."

For a moment Callie stood there, wondering how her voice really sounded. A tiny green hummingbird, with wings that vibrated like an insect's, swooped down beside her. It hung in the air a moment, then darted into the drooping leaves of a nearby tree.

Finally Callie asked, "Have you lived here long?" As soon as she spoke she decided that was a stupid question. Just because she'd moved to Tucson from somewhere else didn't mean everyone else had.

Amy smiled. "I'm a native. One of the few. Tucson's funny that way; the city's grown so fast that not many of the people who live here now were born here. Old Mrs. Hansen, the lady you bought your house from, is another native. Mrs. Hansen only moved away because she had to go into a nursing home, you know; she's been here for as long as anyone can remember. I think her parents were born here, too. I'm told they lived on the land back when it was still a ranch. That was a long time ago, of course."

Callie hadn't known the land had once been a ranch. She looked around, trying to imagine cattle and sheep instead of houses. Even with the dirt road, she couldn't quite picture it.

A sudden movement across the street caught Callie's eye—a gray blur by the side of her new house, near the screened patio. She saw a flick of a tail, heard the stamp of a hoof, and then the horse disappeared around back.

"Hey, did you see that?" Callie asked.

"See what?" Amy said.

Callie looked across the street again; the horse was nowhere in sight. Maybe she hadn't really seen it at all. Maybe she'd just wanted it to be there so badly, she'd convinced herself she had.

"Nothing," Callie said. "I thought I saw a horse, but I guess I imagined it."

Amy grinned. "Horses are cool. My brother, Josh, works at a stable, and I get to ride whenever business is slow. Riding's almost as much fun as reading."

To work with horses for a living—now that would be neat. Callie wanted to ask Amy more about her brother, but then she heard someone calling her. Mom stood by the house, waving Callie inside.

Callie sighed. "I'd better go," she said. She quickly added, "But maybe we can get together sometime."

"Sure," Amy said. "That'd be fun."

Callie ran across the street, turning once to wave at Amy as she went. Amy waved back, then sat down in front of her house and continued reading.

Even though they'd only just met, Callie liked Amy. Maybe they would become friends. Meeting Amy didn't make up for Callie's having to leave her friends behind in New York, but it did make the fact a little bit easier to bear.

Mom wanted Callie to help clean the house; she handed Callie a mop and set her to work in the kitchen. Melissa, claiming she'd already done her share, was sprawled out on the living room carpet with a magazine.

Callie mopped as fast as she could. Then she hurried back outside, through the kitchen door to the patio. She still feared she'd imagined the horse she saw earlier, and even if she hadn't, it was probably gone by now. Still, she had to look for it. Just to be sure.

There was no horse by the side of the house. Callie stared out into the trees, but she didn't see a horse there, either. On one of the branches, a gray bird cooed loudly; out of sight, another bird answered it.

Callie hesitated. Then she bit her lip and ran around the patio, into the backyard. As she ran she felt the same strange tingling as she had the night before, a prickling down her spine and along her arms and legs.

A horse stood in the yard, staring at her bedroom window. Callie caught her breath. The horse was real; Callie hadn't dreamed it after all.

She was a beautiful mare, even more stunning by daylight than by moonlight. Her coat was more gray than silver, but it was a rich, shimmery gray that shone in the sun. The mark on her forehead was bright white. She had a wonderful lightness about her, as if she shouldn't quite be able to stay on the ground— and surely when she moved her hooves would fly free.

Callie was afraid to breathe, afraid that the slightest sound would make the horse dissolve into the shimmering heat. She approached from behind, very slowly, cringing at the sound of her feet against the loose dirt.

The horse's ears twitched back, as if startled by something. Callie stopped short. The horse's skin rippled beneath her gray coat. She stamped one hoof against the dirt. Her ears went flat against her head.

Some instinct made Callie jump away. She hit the ground, hard, just as the mare kicked backward where she'd been. Dust flew up, clogging Callie's throat and nose. She started coughing. She heard hooves clomping against the ground as the horse ran away. By the time she could breathe again, Callie knew it was gone.

The sandy dirt burned through Callie's T-shirt. She got to her knees, wincing as she put weight on them, then stood up. Her jeans were torn, her shins scratched and caked with blood and dirt. She looked around, but she didn't see any sign of the horse at all—not even hoofprints to tell her which way it had gone.

She'd seen it running, though. Running away from her.

Callie scowled. Let it run away, she told herself. If the horse didn't want anything to do with her, she didn't want anything to do with it, either. She didn't care what happened to it at all.

As soon as Callie thought that, though, she knew it wasn't true. She did care, even as she tried to convince herself she didn't. More than anything, she wanted the horse to come back. It was the first truly beautiful thing she'd seen since coming to the desert.

Of course, the horse wasn't hers to want back in the first place. The horse had probably run home to her real owner, whoever that was. Callie would probably never see her again.

Knowing that something so beautiful and special wanted nothing to do with her hurt Callie much more than her scratched shins.

Chapter Three

Callie hoped no one would notice her torn jeans and bloody knees, but of course she had no such luck. As she walked around to the front of the house, she saw Melissa standing outside, beneath the shade of the awning, talking to a tall boy. Melissa glanced at Callie's torn jeans and then looked quickly away, as if embarrassed to be seen with someone who was such a mess.

Callie bit her lip. She wanted to run into the house and hide, but before she could, the boy held out a hand and said, "Hi there. I'm Josh."

"I'm Callie." She shook the boy's hand, all the while wishing she could sink into the ground and disappear. Then the boy's name registered. "You're Amy's brother, aren't you? The one who works with horses?" Probably *he* had never almost been kicked. Probably horses never ran away from him, either. Callie was suddenly jealous.

"That's me." Josh grinned. He was older than Amy, around college age, but he had the same thin, lanky build. His hair was blond, and curls of it spilled onto his shoulders. A battered straw hat dangled from his neck down his back. His eyes were blue and very deep, like the cloudless sky behind him. Callie glanced at her scraped knees, feeling suddenly young and uncomfortable.

Josh shoved his hands into the pockets of his jeans. "It's good to see kids Amy's age here."

"Well," Melissa said, tossing her head, "I'm probably too old for your sister, but I'm sure Callie and Amy will get along just fine."

"What's that supposed to mean?" Callie felt her cheeks turn hot. Why did Melissa have to turn everything she did into something embarrassing?

Josh shrugged, then glanced at his watch. "Well, like I was saying, I really do have to get back to work. See you girls later?"

"Of course." Melissa smiled her most syrupy smile.

"Yeah." Callie didn't look up at him—or at Melissa.

She didn't realize until after Josh was gone that she hadn't even had a chance to ask him about horseback riding.

When Callie went inside, she had to explain her dirty clothes and torn jeans to her parents. She told them she'd fallen while out in the yard, but she didn't tell them how. They didn't ask.

"We can't be graceful all the time," Mom said. She always said things like that. Callie knew Mom was trying to make her feel better, but she only felt worse. Maybe she really was just a kid, like Melissa always said. Melissa never got dirty, after all, or tore her clothes or scraped her knees. Callie pushed the thought fiercely aside and changed out of her dirty—and by now sweaty—clothes.

They ate dinner late that night. Mom didn't want pizza again, and Dad got lost trying to find a grocery store. By the time they were done, Callie was exhausted. As soon as she and Melissa finished washing the dishes (they ate on paper plates, so there were only a few pans to wash), Callie went to her room.

Mom had sprayed the room with some sort of deodorizer, but the mothbally smell was still there. Now the mothballs were rose-scented, but Callie wasn't sure that was an improvement.

Callie sighed. She climbed into bed and kicked off her shoes, too tired to change into pajamas. She fell asleep to the smell of mothballs and the sound of yipping in the darkness.

As she slept, Callie dreamed.
She saw the silver-gray mare, tied to a metal rail. The horse stood behind a house that

looked a lot like Callie's new house, in a yard that looked a lot like her new yard. Only the fences weren't rusted in this yard, and there weren't any other houses—just scrubby trees, cacti, and dry grass, filling hilly fields that stretched all the way to the gray mountains.

In the distance, cattle grazed on the grass— and occasionally on the less spiny cacti. Closer in, a cluster of squawking chickens pecked at the ground. Where the trampled dirt had been in Callie's yard, here there was a full-fledged corral, surrounded by an uneven wood-and-metal fence.

The morning was chilly, the sun not yet above the horizon. Out of sight, a bird warbled. The horse pawed the ground and snorted, blowing out frosty puffs of steam. Her silvery coat was sleek in the thin morning light. Somehow Callie knew she was dreaming, but she shivered, feeling the cool dawn right along with the horse. She'd never had a dream that felt this vivid before.

"Star!" someone called. The horse turned in the direction of that voice, toward the house.

A boy ran around the side of the house. He was wearing high boots, worn jeans, a long-sleeved shirt, and a floppy leather cowboy hat. His face was tan, and brown hair fell into his eyes. He carried a saddle. Callie saw him at the same moment the horse did. She felt the horse's excitement as the boy approached.

When he reached the horse he dumped the saddle on the ground, beside a battered old saddle blanket, and threw his arms around the horse's neck. The horse didn't run from him, but stood still and let him hold her. The boy stroked the horse's smooth coat, ran his fingers through her mane. Dream or not, Callie was jealous.

She watched him blanket and saddle the horse, walking from one side to the other without getting kicked. She watched him jump into the saddle with one smooth motion. She watched him ride. He and the horse fell into the same liquid rhythm, as if they were one creature.

More than anything, Callie wanted to ride like that.

Horse and boy rode down to the sandy gully, crossing it to the hilly fields. They rode through tall yellow grass and around scraggly bushes, past fuzzy cacti, paddle-shaped cacti, and now and then a tall, branched cactus. Birds chirped loudly back and forth as the sun rose over the mountains. A snub-nosed animal that looked like a hairy pig darted across their path. The horse's ears pricked forward, but she kept a steady pace.

After they'd walked for a while, the boy tightened his legs around the mare ever so slightly, and she broke into a run. They raced through the hills together, past small clusters of grazing cattle, toward the mountains. Wind blew the horse's mane about, blew the boy's hair back from his face. Callie felt the joy that bubbled in the horse as she ran.

Then a man's voice cut through the morning, gravelly and harsh. "Michael!" A gray-haired man rode up beside them. With his hat and boots, he seemed like a grizzled old cowboy out of some movie. He looked tired. The horse he rode looked tired, too, with dull brown eyes that stared at the ground more than anything else.

The boy—Michael—sighed. He leaned back in the saddle, and the horse came to a halt. She stamped one hoof against the ground, eager to move again.

The old man pulled hard on his horse's reins, coming to a sharp stop beside the boy. "Have you got the water pump fixed yet, Michael?"

Michael brushed a hand across his face. "No, Grampa."

"Then what are you doing out so early? Checking on the cattle?"

Michael shook his head, avoiding his grandfather's angry gaze. "I was riding."

"Riding where? And to do what?"

"Just riding."

The man's voice turned harsher. "Well, why

don't you 'just feed the chickens' or 'just milk the cows'? There's work to be done. You're fourteen. That's too old to waste time like this. Understand?"

"Yes, sir."

"Go home and make yourself useful, then."

Michael bit his lip. He blinked once, hard, as if trying not to cry. The horse stamped her foot again. Callie knew that the mare wanted, more than anything, to continue running through the fields. Instead she turned around and started toward home.

After only a few steps, she stopped and turned her head back toward Michael's grandfather. The man had dismounted; he stood on the ground watching them. His face was less angry than before, and more sad.

"Don't you look at me like that," he told the mare. "The work has to be done. That isn't my fault."

Michael pulled on the reins, and the horse turned her head back around. She started walking once more. Even though she and Michael rode slowly now, their movement was every bit as graceful as before. Around them, morning sun bathed the fields in gold light.

How, Callie wondered, could anyone call riding like that a waste of time?

Chapter Four

Callie woke in the darkness of her own room. She felt strangely sad; for a moment she didn't know why. Then she remembered her dream: the horse's sleek hide and smooth gait, the boy who rode her so gracefully, and the boy's grandfather, who was angry at them both. Now that she was awake, the grandfather's anger made even less sense.

Usually Callie didn't remember her dreams, or else she forgot them soon after waking. This dream was different, though; it grew more real and more vivid the longer she thought about it. Even though she knew it was the middle of the night, as she lay in bed she half expected to see the sun really rising, casting yellow light about her room.

The night remained stubbornly dark, though. And cool. For once Callie wasn't hot, even though her window was open.

Callie blinked. She hadn't meant to leave the window open all day. She should close it, especially since she heard the low hum of the air-conditioning. She sat up in bed, swinging her feet around to the floor. As soon as she stood, tingles shot down her spine.

Callie caught her breath, afraid to hope the strange horse had returned. She walked slowly across the room. She knelt by the window, hands trembling as she clutched the sill. She looked outside.

Dark horse eyes stared back at her.

The mare stood just inches from the window; she glistened bright silver in the moonlight. A lock of mane fell onto her forehead, half obscuring the white star below. Callie couldn't stop staring at her. The horse's tail swung impatiently back and forth, as if she was waiting for Callie to join her outside.

Callie tugged at the window screen. Her hand slipped and her knuckles jammed into the window frame. Pain shot through her hand. She glared at the screen and saw that it was rusted in place.

Callie feared the horse would disappear if she let it out of her sight. But she turned away from the window and started toward the kitchen door.

The cool night air felt good against Callie's face and arms. The moon was past full, but it still shone so brightly that she could see the backyard perfectly. Across the yard, an owl hooted. Farther away, she heard a hissing, rattling noise. Something slithered off into the darkness. She shivered but kept walking.

The horse was still staring at the window. She turned at the sound of Callie's footsteps. This time she wore a saddle and a bridle.

Callie took a deep breath. She approached from the front this time, stepping slowly forward until she stood just inches from the mare's nose. The animal had a comfortable, horsy smell, like sweet grass. She snorted softly, blowing warm breath into Callie's face.

Callie laughed. "That tickles!" Something about the horse—a rippling of her coat, a pricking of her ears—told Callie that she was laughing, too. Callie stretched out a hand to touch the silvery mane.

She expected the mare to flinch at her touch or, worse, run away. She did neither. She stood very still as Callie moved her fingers across her coat. The mane was rougher and more tangled than Callie expected, at odds with the horse's sleek appearance.

The hair that covered the rest of her body was smooth, though, silky and soft. Callie ran her hands along the mare's neck. She rubbed the top of the horse's head. She even reached beneath the bridle and scratched behind the ears.

All the while the horse watched her with still black eyes. Through those eyes Callie felt something: love so strong she could almost touch it. She'd never felt anything quite like that before, not from her closest friends and definitely not from her family.

Callie threw her arms around the horse's neck. She leaned her cheek against the soft coat.

"I want you to stay here," Callie whispered. "I don't want you to leave me, ever." Even as she spoke she knew that was impossible. The horse had to have an owner, after all, and a home. Callie wasn't sure why it was in her backyard at all. The most she could hope for was that the horse would keep visiting every once in a while.

Callie stepped back. "Where do you live, horse?"

Calling the animal "horse" sounded silly. Wherever she'd come from, she must have a name.

The white star on the horse's forehead shone, bright as the real stars above, almost as bright as the moon. In Callie's dream, the boy had called the horse Star. That was just a dream, of course, and had nothing to do with the horse's real name at all. Yet the name fit somehow.

Callie smiled. "Star it is." The horse snorted again, and Callie added, "If that's okay with you."

Star stamped one hoof against the ground, as if she approved. Callie grinned. Then she threw her arms around the horse's neck once more. She lost track of how long they stood like that. When she finally stepped back again, her eyes caught on the saddle.

Callie had always wanted to ride. Maybe now was her chance. Star turned her head toward Callie, nudging Callie's chest with her nose.

"Do you want to go for a ride?"

Star snorted loudly, as if impatient to get moving.

Callie stroked the saddle. It was smooth, worn leather. Beneath it was an itchy wool blanket. Both blanket and saddle smelled of leather and horse—and, more faintly, of smoke. Where had Star been before coming to the house?

Callie took a deep breath. For a moment she stared at the stirrups, not quite sure where to begin. Then she shrugged and lifted her right foot toward the stirrup. She could barely reach it, and even once she got her foot in place, she had no idea how to lift the rest of her body over the horse. Callie grabbed the edge of the saddle, trying to pull herself up. Instead the saddle slid toward her. Callie reached upward for a better grip. Her foot slid out of the stirrup. Startled, she let go of the saddle—and crashed, butt-first, to the ground.

Callie heard hooves against dirt. She didn't need to look to know that Star was gone.

Callie pounded her fist against the ground,

fighting not to cry. She'd come so close; Star had almost stayed this time. She pounded the ground again, and something spiny and sharp jabbed into her hand. "Ouch!" she yelled. She brought her hand up to her mouth.

She heard human footsteps running across the yard.

"Hey, are you all right?" Melissa asked. There was real concern in her voice. "I was in the kitchen getting something to drink, and when I looked outside I saw you just lying there."

Callie didn't answer. She took a deep breath, but it came out as a choking sob.

"What are you doing out here so late, anyway?" Melissa asked.

"Just leave me alone!" Callie cried. Melissa was the last person she wanted to talk to right now.

"I was only trying to help," Melissa said.

Callie ignored her.

"Well, fine," Melissa snapped. "Just lie there if you want to; see if I care. Don't bother to thank me or anything just because I ran out in the middle of the night. I'm going back to bed."

Callie waited until Melissa walked away. Then she stood. Her whole body ached.

The moon had dipped behind the house. Dawn had begun for real, and pale yellow light spread across the sky. In the distance birds chirped loudly. Callie looked across the yard, toward the gully and the houses beyond it. She didn't see any hoofprints, but she knew that was the direction Star had gone.

Callie bit her lip. Star had returned before. Would she, just maybe, come back again?

If she did, Callie had to be ready. She had to make sure next time that Star didn't run away.

Chapter Five

By the time Callie went back inside, Melissa was in her room. Her door was closed, but she wasn't sleeping; Callie heard her moving around. Mom and Dad were asleep; Callie heard soft breathing from their bedroom.

Callie moved silently through the house, afraid that her parents might wake up and realize she'd been out so late. She walked into the bathroom and washed the dirt from her hands and arms. Then she went back into her room, closed the window, and crawled into bed. She fell asleep quickly, and this time she didn't dream.

Loud voices and heavy footsteps woke her. It must be the movers, Callie thought, bringing the rest of their things. She pulled the sleeping bag over her head. She felt as though she'd hardly slept at all.

Someone pounded on her door. "Callie?" Dad called. "Can you give us a hand out here?"

Callie groaned and tossed the sleeping bag

off. She stood, rubbing the grit out of her eyes. She dressed quickly and stumbled out of her room, still not quite awake.

Their couch already sat in the living room, along with a couple of cushioned chairs. Two men in jeans and T-shirts carried Mom and Dad's mattress through the front door; Callie ducked to let them by. Her own bed would be carried in soon, too. She went back to her bedroom and pulled the mattress off Mrs. Hansen's old bed. She was glad to finally get rid of it. She dragged the mattress into the living room, then stopped to catch her breath. The door was open for the movers; the room felt stuffy and hot.

"Need some help?"

Callie looked up to see Amy standing in the front doorway. Amy brushed her hair back from her face. "Josh and I saw the truck outside. We thought maybe you could use a hand. Actually, I told Josh I thought the movers would handle most of it, but he said it never hurts to ask." Outside, Callie saw Josh talking to Melissa and her parents.

Callie smiled. "If you could grab one end of this mattress, that'd be great."

They carried the old mattress out to the garage, then the bed frame. The air outside was hotter and drier than indoors. The heat seemed to pull all the water out of Callie, leaving her skin dry and her throat scratchy. By the time they were done carrying the bed frame, she was worn out. She went into the kitchen and filled two glasses with ice cubes and water. She and Amy took them out onto the screened kitchen patio.

Someone had set up a couple of folding chairs out there. The girls sat, staring into the trees beyond the patio in silence. In the shade, the heat wasn't quite as bad, but Callie still drank down most of her glass in one gulp. A thin tree with heart-shaped leaves blew in the wind, making a sound like summer rain.

"What a strange tree," Callie said.

Amy followed Callie's gaze. "Oh, that's a cottonwood," Amy said. "Good shade trees." Amy set her glass down on the ground; she'd only taken a few sips. Callie wondered if she was used to the heat.

Callie looked at the thin branches. The leaves were half brown, as if dried up by the sun. "I like oaks and maples better."

"Not enough water to grow a maple tree out here," Amy said. "Some folks do anyway, but they really shouldn't."

That made sense, but Callie still missed the tall, cool trees of home.

She looked around. She didn't know what to call any of the trees that grew here. She pointed beyond the cottonwood to a tree that had green bark, green branches, and no leaves. "What's that?"

"Palo verde," Amy said. "Since their bark is green, they can drop their leaves when the weather gets too hot. Leaves tend to lose a lot of water."

"Everything here depends on water, doesn't it?"

Amy shrugged. "Well, this is a desert."

"What about the cacti?" Callie pointed beyond the palo verde to a cluster of fuzzy, spiny plants.

"That's cholla," Amy said, "spelled with two *l*'s but pronounced with a *y*. It isn't as cuddly as it looks." She grinned, then pointed to another cactus that looked like a bunch of paddles stuck together. "That one's prickly pear. It grows like a weed out here."

"What about the tall cacti?" Callie asked. "The ones you always see in pictures?"

"Saguaro," Amy said. "Arizona's the only place they grow. Well, here and in parts of Mexico."

Callie wondered whether all the strange things that grew here would ever seem normal. She was silent a moment, listening to the wind rustling through the cottonwood tree. The wind picked up, blowing heat through the screen. Callie finished her water. If June was this hot, what were July and August like?

Janni Lee Simner

"So why'd you decide to move to Arizona?" Amy asked.

Callie told Amy about Mom's computer company moving and about Dad's architecture firm transferring him.

"What do your parents do?" Callie asked.

Amy looked away, as if suddenly embarrassed. She picked up a loose stick and began tracing large circles on the patio floor. She was silent so long, Callie thought maybe she'd decided not to answer. Then Amy said, very low, "Mom and Dad were killed in a car crash. Almost three years ago now. Josh and I live alone."

"Oh." Callie didn't know what to say. Even though her parents drove her crazy, she couldn't imagine them not being there. Just thinking about it made her stomach hurt.

"I'm sorry." Callie felt as though she ought to say something more, but she didn't know what. For a while she and Amy sat without speaking. A line of brown birds, with funny plumes on top of their heads, strutted past the patio door. Callie reached for her water glass again and remembered it was empty.

A sudden sound—loud snorting, the sort only a horse could make—made Callie look up. For a moment she didn't see anything. Then, under one of the palo verde trees, she noticed a flicker of gray. A moment later she saw Star beside the tree, coat and mane shining, tail swishing lazily back and forth. Callie didn't know why she hadn't seen her sooner. Maybe because the sun in Tucson at midday was so much brighter than back home.

The horse stared at Callie. Her steady gaze was calming. Callie forgot her thirst, forgot the heat, forgot the awkwardness that had settled between her and Amy. She once again felt the horse's love, like something real and solid that stretched between them. She wanted to run out and throw her arms around Star's neck, but feared that the movement, like everything else, would make Star run away.

"What are you looking at?" Amy asked. "Another tree?"

"No, the horse." Callie smiled. "Isn't she beautiful?"

"What are you talking about?" Amy squinted and shielded her eyes against the sun. "I don't see anything."

"Right there." Callie pointed. Star turned away and started chewing on some dry grass.

"Right where?"

Why couldn't Amy see what was right in front of her? She was the one used to the bright sun, after all. Callie jumped to her feet to show Amy the horse. The folding chair clattered to the ground behind her. Star's head jerked up at the sound. She looked at Callie again. Then she turned and quietly walked away. For a moment she seemed to shine even brighter than before. Then, all at once, she was gone. She must have disappeared among the other houses.

Amy stood. "There's nothing out there, Callie."

"Not anymore." Callie didn't try to hide her frustration—not only with Amy, but also with Star for leaving.

"Have you been out in the heat too long?" Amy asked. "Or is this just some sort of joke?"

"It's not a joke!" Callie said. Was Amy pretending not to see Star? "There was a horse right there!"

"Callie"—Amy's voice turned suddenly strange and low, yet every bit as angry as Callie's—"I know what's real and what's not real, whatever some people might think. There was no horse out there." Amy opened the patio door and stepped outside the house without another word.

Callie ran after her, back into the bright, hot sunlight. She knew she hadn't done anything wrong. Why was Amy upset with her? Then again, sometimes Callie did everything right and people still got annoyed. She knew that well enough from her family.

Callie followed Amy around to the front of the house. Melissa and Josh stood in the shade of the moving truck, talking. Well, Josh was talking; Melissa was giggling and gazing up at him a lot. Callie should have guessed that Melissa would already be flirting. Back in New York, she'd had high school guys after her, even though she was still in middle school. In the fall Melissa would start high school herself, but Josh was college age at least, maybe a little older. That didn't stop Melissa, though.

Amy walked up to Josh. Callie followed. A tiny gray lizard ran along the edge of the truck, then disappeared inside. It seemed there were lizards everywhere. Maybe they coped with heat better than people did.

Melissa gave Callie a short, sharp look, one that said without words to get lost. Callie stayed anyway. The look disappeared before anyone else noticed.

"What's up?" Amy asked her brother. She didn't look at Callie.

"Not much," Josh said. "Melissa, have you met my sister yet? Amy, this is Melissa."

Melissa smiled. "Nice to meet you. Josh and I were just talking about going for a horseback ride sometime soon."

"We were thinking about it," Josh said quickly. For all of Melissa's flirting, he didn't seem all that interested in her. "The stables are usually pretty quiet in summer. All the winter tourists are gone, and lots of the folks who live here leave to escape the heat, too. Still, I need to check my schedule, and—"

"Can I come, too?" Callie blurted. Josh knew all about horses. If he showed Callie some of the basics, maybe she'd figure out what she was doing wrong with Star.

"I don't think you were invited," Melissa said in a sweet but very fake voice. What she meant, of course, was that she wanted to go with Josh alone.

"Let's all go," Amy said. "It'll be fun to show you Easterners some *real* horses." Amy glanced at Callie. Callie quickly looked away. Star was real, whether Amy admitted it or not.

Josh's face brightened. "Now that'd be fun. When are you guys free?"

"Today," Callie said at once.

"I'm sure Josh is too busy to take all of us on such short notice," Melissa said.

"No, that's fine," Josh said. He seemed to have forgotten about checking his schedule, or maybe he really didn't want to go with Melissa alone. Maybe her flirting looked as silly to him as it did to Callie. "Want to meet at the stables around six-thirty?" Josh asked.

"Sure," Callie said.

"After we check with Mom and Dad, of course." Melissa's voice was still sweet, but her eyes were dark.

"Great." Josh glanced at his watch. "I have

to get back to work; the stables close at midday, when it's too hot to ride, but open again in the late afternoon. I'll see you guys later, okay?"

Callie nodded. Melissa smiled. Josh crossed the street to his house, climbed into a blue hatchback, and drove away.

As soon as he was gone Melissa cast a sour look at Callie. "Thanks for ruining everything!" Melissa turned away and stormed into the house, slamming the door shut behind her.

"What's her problem?" Amy asked.

"I think she likes your brother," Callie said. "I think she wanted to be alone with him."

"Your sister—and Josh?" Amy started laughing. "He's too old for her! Besides, Josh is my brother. Why would anyone—" Amy laughed harder. Her laughter was contagious; soon Callie started laughing, too. Somehow Melissa seemed less annoying when Callie could laugh at her.

Neither Callie nor Amy mentioned their argument, or Star, for the rest of the day.

Chapter Six

Mom and Dad quickly agreed to let Callie and Melissa go riding, saying they were glad to see the girls making friends. Dad drove Callie, Melissa, and Amy down to the stables, which turned out to be the same Sonoran Stables they'd driven past when they first arrived in Tucson.

The first thing Callie noticed as she stepped out of the car was the smell of the horses. It was stronger and sweatier than Star's scent had been. Melissa smelled it, too; she scrunched her face and put a hand over her nose.

Josh greeted them at the car and handed Dad a release form. Callie glanced over her father's shoulder at it. The form said that riding, like all sports, was sometimes dangerous, and that Sonoran Stables wasn't responsible for any injuries. Callie rubbed her knees, which were still sore from when she'd fallen. She already knew horses could be dangerous. She still wanted to ride. She wandered away from Dad, toward the horses.

Callie had expected the stables to look the way they did in movies, with red wooden barn stalls lined up neatly side by side. Instead the horses stood in stalls that were open on all sides, bounded only by shoulder-high metal fences, with flat tin roofs overhead. The fences reminded Callie of the rusted metal fences in her new backyard. If her house had really been part of a ranch, there had probably been horses there once, too.

Behind the stalls, the mountains stretched toward the sky. No matter where Callie went, she couldn't seem to get away from those mountains.

The stable horses were all colors, from white to brown, red to black, speckled to almost solid. They were beautiful, though none was half as gorgeous as Star. One cream-colored gelding walked right up to the rail of his stall, nudging Callie's chest with his wet nose.

"That's disgusting," Melissa said.

"No, it isn't," Callie told her. Callie turned to face Melissa just as Dad and Josh walked up behind her sister. Dad hugged the girls good-bye, told them to have fun riding, and headed back to the car.

"Come on," Josh said. He held the release forms in one hand. "I'll check you guys in." He led the girls to a low wooden shack. Behind her, Callie heard Dad drive away.

Once they were inside, Josh handed them riding helmets. The white plastic reminded Callie of her bicycle helmet. Then he left to get the horses; the girls followed him back outside. Amy removed her hat and pulled on her helmet, fastening the strap under her chin. Callie did the same.

"Oh, gross," Melissa muttered as she walked. She lifted a booted foot out of a pile of manure. "My shoe's ruined." Melissa wore a pair of fringed black suede boots. Callie was glad she'd worn her old tennis shoes and battered jeans.

Josh returned leading two horses; an older woman followed with one more. Josh handed the reins of one—a brown horse with white speckles—to Amy. Amy jumped into the saddle as easily as the boy had in Callie's dream.

"That is, of course, harder than it looks," Josh said. "You two might want to use a mounting block."

"Oh, I don't need that," Melissa said lightly. Callie wondered if she was trying to impress Josh.

Josh just shrugged. "Go on over to Mary, then." He indicated the woman holding the other horse. "She'll help you out."

He turned to Callie. "How about you?"

Callie looked at the horse Josh held. It was deep brown, with a black mane and tail. It was also taller than Star.

"I'll use the mounting block," she said.

Josh led the horse up to a low wooden step. "In spite of all appearances, your horse's name is Tiny." Josh turned the left stirrup around backward. "Step onto the block, then put your left foot up right here."

Callie did so.

"Now, hold Tiny's mane with one hand, his saddle with the other, and swing yourself into place."

Callie grabbed the saddle and tried to jump up. She couldn't jump high enough. She tried to pull herself up instead. She couldn't pull high enough, either, and she felt the saddle slide toward her. She tried pushing instead, propelling her body up over the horse. The stirrup swung forward, Callie swung upward, and her right foot cleared the horse's back. All at once, she fell into place on top of the saddle.

"Not bad," Josh said.

Callie grinned. For the first time in her life, she was really on a horse. Now she just had to remember how to do the same thing the next time she saw Star.

Her legs felt awkward, pushed outward by the saddle and pulled inward by the stirrups, but otherwise Callie felt pretty comfortable. In front of her, a horn stuck up from the saddle. Callie grabbed it with one hand; with the other she reached out to stroke Tiny's neck. His coat was soft, though not quite as silky as Star's.

Josh lifted the reins over Tiny's head and handed them to Callie. "Hold them in one hand," he said. "Keep your other hand by your side; don't use the horn unless you have to. Tiny will usually follow the horses in front of him, but if you need to turn, just pull the reins in the direction you want to go. If you need to stop, pull back. Also pull back if your horse tries to munch on the local plant life." Josh grinned and patted Tiny on the shoulder. "He's already been fed this afternoon.

"If he stops, just give him a little kick. That's not the best way to make a horse move, and if you were one of my students, I'd teach you more subtle ways to ride. But for a trail ride, it'll do."

Someone yelled. Callie twisted around. Melissa was gripping her horse's saddle with both hands, one foot in the stirrups, the other swinging helplessly above the ground. "Just let me try one more time," Melissa sputtered.

The woman beside her shook her head. She dropped the reins, cupped her hands beneath Melissa's loose foot, and pushed. Melissa landed in the saddle with a thud.

"Thanks," Melissa said, but her face was red with embarrassment.

"I'll get Rusty," Josh said, "and then we can go."

Amy pulled her horse up beside Callie. She looked completely at ease in the saddle, tall and straight, but not at all stiff. "Rusty is Josh's horse," Amy said. "I mean, he owns him and all." Amy reached forward and patted her horse on the shoulder. "I want my own horse one day, too."

"Yeah," Callie agreed, "that'd be neat." Callie knew which horse she wanted, but she doubted Star was for sale. How could anyone sell a horse like that?

Josh returned riding a coppery red gelding. "We'll be gone about an hour," he told Mary. Then he clicked his tongue, squeezed his legs tighter around his horse, and started moving.

Callie pulled her heels out to kick Tiny, but he started forward on his own. His walk was rougher than she expected; the saddle rubbed uncomfortably against her tailbone. Still, it was fun to feel Tiny walking beneath her. It was fun to be on horseback at last.

Melissa fell into place behind Josh, Callie behind Melissa. Amy brought up the rear.

For a few minutes the horses followed a wide dirt road; then they turned onto a narrower trail. Tiny sighed as he hit the trail. His steps turned slow and deliberate as he picked his way around rocks and small bushes.

The trail climbed slowly into the mountains, which Josh said were called the Catalinas. Callie was struck yet again by how different the Catalinas were from the Catskills, the mountains closest to Long Island.

The plants around them grew thicker: saguaro, taller and closer together than near the house; clusters of prickly pear; fuzzy yellow-green cholla; a gnarled, small-leaved tree that Amy said was called a mesquite. Tiny reached down to chew on some grass. Callie pulled on the reins. Tiny snorted. He started to walk again, very slowly, as if he'd rather not move at all. A gap grew between him and Melissa's horse. Callie kicked Tiny, but he wouldn't go any faster.

"Oh, stop being grumpy," Amy called from behind them. It took Callie a moment to realize Amy was talking to Tiny, not to her. "You'll have enough to eat when you get home. There's no excuse to drag your feet now."

Callie turned to look at Amy. "You're sure he's not really hungry?" she asked.

"Nah. Grazing's sort of an instinct with horses. They don't know when to stop eating; if there's something around to munch on, they want it. And this"—Amy gestured to the plants along the trail—"is one big salad bar as far as a horse is concerned."

Callie had a sudden, crazy image of Tiny wandering through a salad bar, plate held delicately between his teeth. She laughed. "What kind of dressing do horses prefer?" she asked, not really expecting an answer.

"Ranch, of course," Amy said. They both burst into giggles.

Still laughing, Callie turned forward and kicked Tiny again. If anything, he walked even slower.

"He's in a mood," Amy said.

"Maybe I'm doing something wrong." Callie watched Tiny's feet slowly hit the ground, one after another. If she was a better rider, he'd listen to her, wouldn't he?

"Actually, it's probably both of you," Amy said. "I mean, your balance isn't perfect, but it's good enough for a beginner. And you're handling the reins well enough. Sometimes horses just have bad days. Same as people."

Callie looked ahead. A few feet in front of her, Melissa clutched her reins tightly with both hands. In front of Melissa, Josh looked perfectly at ease. Callie glanced back at Amy. Amy looked comfortable, too, reins held loosely in one hand, the other hand dangling by her side. "I can't picture a horse ever having a bad day around you or Josh," Callie said.

"That's because you've never seen Josh get kicked," Amy said with a laugh. "Just last week he was trying to break in this young gelding, and—"

"Hey!" Josh whirled around to face them; his horse kept its eyes on the trail and continued walking. "That wasn't my fault!"

"Of course not." Amy kept laughing.

"You'd better watch out," Josh said. "I just might tell about the first time you ever set eyes on a horse. You tried to sneak up on it, all quiet and gentle. Nearly scared the poor thing out of its skin."

"I was just a kid then," Amy said. "How was I supposed to know that horses can't see what's directly behind them? I didn't know how easily horses spook, either."

Callie blinked. So that's what she'd done wrong with Star the first time—snuck up on her from behind. The horse had been frightened; that was why she'd kicked.

The very idea that two experienced riders could have a hard time with horses made Callie feel better. Maybe there was still hope that she'd figure out how to ride Star.

They continued riding. The horses were slick with sweat, but the air had slowly begun to cool. They followed the trail upward, along the ridge of a hill, climbing until a wall of rock towered to their right. In the late afternoon sun, the rock shimmered orange. Callie stared up at it until she felt dizzy.

To Callie's left, the rocks fell sharply away. Tucson lay spread out on the flat desert floor below; beyond the city, Callie saw more mountains. In the fading light, the buildings glowed. Tucson was much prettier from up here than from down in the valley.

Callie looked to her right again. The rocks were now washed in pink, shimmery light. "It's beautiful," Callie said.

"Is it safe?" Melissa stared at the drop toward Tucson.

Josh shrugged. "The horses know what they're doing. Just don't get in their way."

As if in response, Melissa's horse stopped short and took a bite from the nearest tree. Tiny and Callie quickly caught up with them, while Josh pulled farther ahead.

From behind Callie, Amy called out, "Pull on the reins."

"I'm trying!" Melissa tugged on her horse's reins, first gently, than more strongly, but he kept eating. Melissa kicked him, hard.

Without warning, the horse threw his head back and ran. Melissa screamed.

Josh whirled around to face her. "Your reins!" he yelled. Melissa ignored him. The reins flew from her hands and she clutched the saddle horn instead. Her horse didn't stop until he caught up with Josh. Then he skidded to a halt, so abruptly that pebbles flew out from beneath his hooves.

Josh jumped out of the saddle and hurried to Melissa's side. "You okay?"

Melissa's face was white. "I could have been killed!"

Amy laughed. "That was just a trot. You should see him when he gets to cantering or galloping."

Josh gave Amy a dark look. Then he turned back to Melissa. "You did fine. It's always frightening the first time a horse bolts. You stayed in the saddle, and that's all that matters. Ready to go on now?"

Melissa didn't answer, but when Josh handed her the reins, she took them. Josh mounted his horse and started forward again. Melissa's horse followed. Melissa didn't say anything more for the rest of the ride.

Tiny continued plodding along. The sun dipped beneath the horizon. The color drained from the rocks, leaving them gray once more. A dark bird flew jaggedly back and forth; it took Callie a moment to realize it was really a bat.

As soon as the stables came into sight, Tiny lifted his head. For the first time, Callie felt a hint of enthusiasm in his steps. He walked faster, as if all he'd cared about all along was getting back home.

Callie sighed. "Don't you enjoy riding, Tiny?" she asked. Tiny just continued his eager walk.

At the stables, Josh helped Callie dismount. Swinging off the horse was much easier than swinging on. Callie's knees, as she hit the ground, felt wobbly, but otherwise she was fine. She looked back toward the mountains. They were little more than outlines against a pale sky. Above the peaks, the first stars twinkled. The mountains didn't seem ugly at all now.

Tiny cheerfully let Josh lead him away. Callie watched them go.

"I'm never doing *that* again," Melissa said. Her face was still pale, her hands trembling. She seemed to have completely forgotten about impressing Josh.

Callie smiled. She was riding again, first chance she got—and, she hoped, on a horse more enthusiastic than Tiny. Maybe even that night.

Chapter Seven

Mom drove Callie and Melissa home. Amy stayed at the stables with Josh; she said she'd catch a ride back with him later.

Melissa didn't speak during the drive. Callie did all the talking. She told Mom about the horses, about the mountains, about the sunset.

"I'm glad to hear you had fun," Mom said. "I knew you'd like Tucson if you gave it a chance."

Callie bristled. She hadn't said she liked Tucson, and she hadn't said she was glad they'd moved. She'd just said she liked riding through the mountains. She stared out the window, watching the houses go by.

The dusty brown and gray buildings were less depressing than before. After seeing Tucson from above, the city seemed less ugly from below. Callie didn't admit that, though. Instead she turned to Mom and asked, "Can I take riding lessons?"

"I'll have to discuss it with your father first," Mom said, not committing to anything—but not saying no, either. Callie thought that maybe she would try talking to both of them at dinner.

They drove the rest of the way home in silence, reaching the house as the pale twilight faded to midnight blue. The moving truck was gone. In the living room Callie found their furniture, from the color TV to their cushioned orange couch, from the wooden end tables to the rocking chair Mom sometimes read in.

In her bedroom she found her own bed; someone had made it up with clean sheets and her thin summer blanket. She collapsed face first onto the mattress.

When Callie stood again, the insides of her legs ached in protest. They'd felt okay during the ride, but now they were stiff. She stretched one leg, then the other, trying to work the soreness out. Then she looked around.

Her dresser leaned against one wall; an overstuffed chair sat in the corner. The rest of the room was filled with boxes. Most of them contained her things, but the boxes in the closet were the ones the old owner had left behind. Callie wished Mrs. Hansen would take them away already. Since she had to live here, she wanted to make the room hers as quickly as she could.

Callie looked at the peeling wallpaper, at the yellowing linoleum floor. Until the room was painted and carpeted, it wouldn't feel right. She wondered how anyone had ever been able to live there. Maybe Mrs. Hansen had just used the room for storage or something.

Callie glanced at the window. Now that it was closed, the room was chilly, the air-conditioning running full blast.

Maybe Star already stood outside. Maybe Callie could try to ride her right away. She felt her heart beating hard in her chest. She hurried to the window, knelt beside it, and looked out.

The sky was black, the yard empty. A huge yellow moon rose over the mountains.

Callie sighed. Just because Star had been outside the past few times wasn't any reason to expect her that night. Probably she was at home with her real owner. Maybe she wasn't going to return at all. Callie swallowed hard, fighting tears at the thought.

"Callie!" Mom called. "Dinner!"

"I'm not hungry!" Callie called back, though her stomach rumbled. They were eating later than usual; Mom and Dad had decided to wait until after the ride. Callie couldn't leave now, though. What if Star came by while she was gone?

"Please join us anyway!"

Callie looked out the window again, straining to see Star in the distance. The yard remained empty, all the way out to the gully.

Callie sighed again, then stood and went into the kitchen.

The kitchen table from home was set up now; Melissa and Mom already sat there. Melissa had changed into clean clothes: white shorts, a T-shirt, and sandals.

Dad pulled a casserole from the oven and carried it to the table. Callie sniffed. The casserole smelled of cheese, meat, and broccoli. She hated broccoli. She scooped a small spoonful onto her plate. At Dad's sharp look, she added a second spoonful before passing the dish on.

"Aren't you going to change your clothes?" Melissa whispered. Callie still wore the jeans and old tennis shoes she'd ridden in. "You reek of horse. I couldn't wait to get rid of that smell, myself." Melissa stretched out one leg, than the other. Callie realized she was sore, too.

Mom poured herself a glass of iced tea. "Melissa was telling us about your ride. Sounds to me like it was a bit more dangerous than Josh let on."

"It wasn't dangerous." Callie pushed her food around on her plate. "It was fun."

"Fun?" Melissa choked on a mouthful of casserole. "I was nearly killed!"

"You were not! Josh said you did fine."

Mom ignored her. "Given the way Melissa's horse ran off, I don't really think you girls should—"

Callie's stomach tightened. She knew what Mom was going to say next. Callie spoke quickly, her words tumbling over each other. "He wasn't running very fast, Mom. And he stopped as soon as he caught up with the horse in front of him. Melissa's just being stupid."

Melissa brushed an invisible speck of dust from her shirt. "How would you know how fast he was going? You weren't riding him."

Callie threw her fork down; it clattered against her plate. "If I'd been riding him, he wouldn't have bolted in the first place!" she yelled. "You shouldn't have kicked him like that. It's not my fault you don't like horses—or that they don't like you!"

"Callie!" Dad looked at her across the table. "Please lower your voice and stop insulting your sister."

Callie scowled at her plate. She picked up her fork again and began separating the broccoli from the rest of the casserole.

"As I was saying"—Mom swallowed a mouthful of food—"I didn't realize how dangerous horses were. And I don't like the release form Josh made your father sign, either. While it was very generous of Josh to take you girls riding, I'd prefer you not go again."

"No!" Callie's stomach twisted into knots. She felt like she was going to throw up. How could they ban her from riding, just when she

67

was learning how to do it right? How could they stop her before she even had a chance to ride Star? "It isn't fair!" Callie yelled. "If Melissa doesn't want to ride, that's her problem, but don't stop me, too!"

Dad set his glass down on the table. "If your mother says not to ride, you won't ride." His voice was low and firm. "Now finish your dinner."

"I'm not hungry." Callie stared numbly at her plate, unable to believe she might never ride again. Melissa had ruined everything. And her parents, as always, hadn't even listened to Callie's side of things.

Mom and Dad made her stay at the table. They made her eat everything on her plate, too.

Including the broccoli.

As soon as she finished eating, Callie ran to her room. She slammed the door shut, threw herself down on the bed, and cried.

Why did Melissa have to mess everything up? What did Melissa have against Callie, anyway? For as long as Callie could remember, her sister had always insulted her, or told her she was acting like a child, or tried to get her out of the way completely.

Callie pounded a fist against her mattress. She kicked the edge of her bed frame. She threw a pillow across the room. It bounced off the wall and fell onto a pile of boxes. She reached for another pillow, then stopped abruptly.

By throwing things around, she really was acting like a child. She was proving Melissa right.

Callie took one deep breath, then another. She rolled onto her back and stared at the ceiling. She couldn't stop riding now. Somehow she had to change Mom and Dad's minds.

Callie sighed and closed her eyes. She heard the hum of the air-conditioning. After a long while she heard Mom, Dad, and Melissa talking as they walked toward their bedrooms.

Callie felt herself drifting off to sleep. Her mind wandered, first to her trail ride that day, then to Star. She saw Star trotting beneath a bright moon. She tried to picture herself on Star's back, but instead she saw the boy from her dream, sitting tall and straight in the saddle. It wasn't fair. Even in her dreams she couldn't ride Star.

A tingling ran down her spine, along her arms and legs. What a pleasant way to fall asleep.

A tingling—

Callie bolted upright in bed. Her whole body tingled now. Only two nights earlier, the electric feeling had scared her. Now it was familiar, almost comfortable. Callie jumped out of bed and ran to the window.

Star stood in the yard. She stared through the window with a dark, curious gaze.

"You came back!" Callie cried. She pushed the window open.

Star tossed her head back and snorted. She pressed her nose up to the screen. She wanted Callie to come outside. Callie felt a surge of joy at the thought.

"Wait," Callie said. "I'll be right there."

The hallway outside her room was dark. She heard Mom and Dad walking around in their room. Melissa was in the bathroom, running the shower. Callie crept down the hall and through the kitchen. She cringed as the kitchen door creaked shut behind her.

Mom and Dad had said she couldn't ride. They hadn't said she couldn't be near horses. Still, Callie knew that if they heard her, they'd make her return to her room.

She hurried around the house. Star still stood in the yard, coat glistening silver beneath the waning moon, saddle dark against her body. Tiny was drab in comparison.

Star turned at the sound of Callie's footsteps. Callie threw her arms around the horse's neck. Star nudged Callie's chest with her wet nose. The dampness soaked through her shirt, but she didn't care. She reached up to scratch behind Star's ears. Her hand touched the soft leather of Star's bridle.

A lump formed in Callie's throat. The bridle was a reminder that she couldn't ride, not now and maybe not ever. She stepped back from Star, fighting the tears again. The reins were draped loosely over the saddle horn. More than anything, Callie wanted to ride.

"I can't," Callie whispered to Star. "Mom and Dad won't let me."

Star snorted, blowing warm air into Callie's face. She stamped her foot impatiently. Star didn't know what Mom and Dad had said. Somehow Callie doubted the horse would care.

Callie took a deep breath. Her parents were about to go to sleep. They wouldn't know if she rode, would they? For a moment she felt guilty at the thought. But Mom and Dad were wrong not to let her ride. Callie knew they were.

"Right," she told Star. "Let's give this one more try."

Callie looked around for something to use as a mounting block, but she didn't see anything. She thought about standing on one of the rusty fences, but it would probably give way beneath her feet. This time Callie was determined not to fall.

Callie ran her fingers through her hair. She walked to Star's side, examining the stirrup. Star shifted forward, dragging the stirrup out of Callie's reach.

"Stand still," Callie snapped. "I can't get up there if you move around."

Star stopped moving at once. She stood stone still, as if she'd heard Callie's words and understood them. How much did horses understand, anyway? Callie had had a dog when she was younger, and he'd understood a few words, but not whole sentences.

The first time Callie tried to mount, the saddle slid toward her, just like before. She didn't panic this time; instead she jumped to the ground, straightened the saddle, and tried again. This time she gripped Star's mane instead of the saddle, and she pushed her body forward and upward. She dropped neatly into place on top of Star.

For a moment Callie just sat there, breathing hard. She was on Star's back; she really was. The saddle was softer than the one she'd used earlier, more comfortable. It still smelled faintly of smoke, but it smelled more strongly of leather and horse.

This time Star showed no signs of wanting to run away. Callie reached out and stroked Star's neck. Tingles ran up her arms. The mare turned her head toward Callie. Star whuffled, and Callie knew the horse was as pleased as she was.

Callie looked around. From Star's back she saw well beyond the dry gully. Moonlight reflected off the flat roofs of the houses and lit the outlines of the Catalina Mountains.

Callie remembered her dream. She remembered how gracefully Star and the boy—Michael—had ridden together. She wondered how riding like that would feel. She tried to picture Star moving in the moonlight, all silky and graceful.

All of a sudden Callie really was moving. Star had started walking on her own, without Callie's doing anything. The horse had a smooth, liquid gait that was nothing like the bumpy ride Callie had taken earlier that day. Callie moved with Star, to the exact same rhythm. She felt taller and more graceful than she'd ever felt before. If Melissa saw her now, she wouldn't dare call Callie a little kid.

No, Callie realized. If Melissa saw her now, she'd tell their parents.

Callie tasted panic at the back of her throat. If her parents caught her, they probably wouldn't let her even see Star again, let alone ride. Callie reached for the reins. Before she could pull back on them, Star came to a crisp halt.

Callie stared at the loose reins in her hand. How had Star known she wanted to stop? Callie must have pulled on the reins without realizing it.

Something scuttled through the underbrush. Star stretched her neck and bent her head to the ground, sniffing at a clump of weeds. Callie sighed. She didn't want to stop riding. She wanted to keep going forever.

Star's ears perked up. She lifted her head and started walking again, toward the circle of trampled dirt. It was as if Star had known Callie wanted to move, even though Callie hadn't spoken aloud. That was impossible, though. Maybe Callie had just moved her hands or her legs in a way that told Star what she wanted to do.

Then again, maybe not.

Stop, Callie thought, testing the horse. Star came to the same sharp, clean halt she had before.

Walk. Star started forward once more, following the outline of the dirt circle. Callie gasped. Somehow Star knew her thoughts. She was an even more wonderful horse than Callie had imagined.

Callie wondered what riding faster would feel like. She thought about the way Melissa's horse had broken into a trot.

Star bolted forward. Callie flew upward; she grabbed wildly at the horn to keep from flying out of the saddle. Her hands sweated against the leather. For a moment she understood why Melissa had been so scared.

Callie took a deep breath and forced herself to sit more firmly in the saddle. She lengthened her legs and pulled her back up straighter behind her. She released the horn and held her rein hand slightly in front of it.

That was better. Callie felt more in control now. Trotting wasn't so frightening after all; in fact, it was fun. Star's steps were spirited and fast. There was a hint of something in those steps— laughter. Star was moving for the joy of it. She liked going fast. Callie just knew it. She heard the two-beat rhythm of Star's hooves against the dirt. She heard her own breathless laughter, spilling out into the cool air. Callie liked going fast, too.

She remembered how Star and Michael had run in her dream. The rhythm of their running had been different somehow.

Without warning, Star burst into a faster gait. Callie was nearly thrown from the saddle again. She gripped the horn and regained her balance. Star seemed to roll beneath her. The motion was smoother and less bumpy than a trot, yet also much faster. Callie still heard Star's hooves, but they hit the ground differently, with three beats instead of two. Callie wondered whether this was a canter or a gallop. She'd heard both terms before but had never been sure exactly what they meant.

Whatever it was, Star continued to run. The horse's mane blew wildly about; cool wind brushed Callie's cheek. She felt as though she and Star were one creature, running to the same flowing rhythm.

Sometimes they rode within the circle of trampled dirt; sometimes they rode in larger loops around the yard. Callie lost track of how long she ran. All she knew was that she'd never felt so happy or so alive.

A pale yellow glow above the mountains caught her eye. Had she really been riding all night? She sighed. She knew she had to go inside before her parents woke up again. At least their bedroom window faced away from the backyard, the same as Melissa's did.

"Stop," Callie whispered. It was the hardest thing she'd ever said. Star slowed to a trot, then a walk. She walked right up to Callie's window and stopped there.

Callie swung out of the saddle. Or rather, she tried to. One foot hit the ground, the other got tangled in the stirrup, and she fell to the dirt.

Star had run away the other times when Callie fell.

Callie slowly looked up. Star still stood beside her. The horse's eyes were bright, as if she was ready to ride again. Her tail swished steadily back and forth.

"You stayed," Callie whispered. The horse liked her enough to want to be with her. She smiled at the thought.

She stood, brushing the dirt off her clothes.

Now that she was on the ground again, she felt strangely awkward. Her knees ached, protesting at her sudden weight on them.

She reached up and scratched Star behind the ears. "You'll come back tomorrow, won't you?" she said. She thought about her parents and about the fact that she wasn't supposed to ride at all. "It's not fair," she said. "They have no right to make me stop." She knew that she couldn't give up something this wonderful.

She wouldn't give it up. If Star returned, Callie would ride her.

She'd just have to make sure her parents—and Melissa—didn't find out about it.

Chapter Eight

As she tiptoed back into the house, Callie felt suddenly tired. She changed quickly into pajamas and collapsed into bed. She drifted off to sleep thinking about Star and hoping she'd dream about riding her.

Instead she dreamed about the boy riding Star. That was strange; Callie never dreamed about the same thing two nights in a row. Although she was a little bit annoyed to see the boy riding Star—she wanted the horse to herself—she was curious about him, too.

In the dream, Star stood in the yard that looked like Callie's yard, in a metal stall that looked like the stalls at Sonoran Stables. Star watched Michael pound wooden fence posts into the ground a short distance away. The Tucson afternoon was hot, just like in real life; Callie felt the same relentless afternoon sun that Star did. The sky was clear, deep blue, and cloudless, exactly as it had been every day since Callie had arrived in Tucson. Weren't there ever any clouds? Didn't it ever rain?

Michael pounded the last post into the ground. He set the hammer aside, wiped a sweaty hand across his forehead, and walked over to Star. She stamped her hoof, eager for a ride.

"Not now, Star. I need to string wire between the posts." Michael sighed and looked around; Star followed his gaze. There were horses and chickens near the house, cattle farther out, but no people.

Michael's face broke into a grin. "It's too hot to string wire now, anyway. Let's ride."

Star tossed her head back in approval.

Michael saddled Star, grabbed a canteen full of water, and jumped onto her back. They started away from the house at a walk, breaking into a trot as soon as they reached the fields beyond the gully. Star didn't seem to read Michael's thoughts, not the way she did Callie's, but Michael didn't need to kick her into going faster, either. Instead he tightened his legs around her sides, just as he had in the first dream.

Star and Michael broke from the trot into the faster, three-beat run. Somehow Callie knew for sure now that it was called a canter.

Star and Michael sped up even more, into a fiery, four-beat run. That was a gallop! Michael's hat flew from his head and hung down his back by the strap. Wind blew Star's mane into her eyes and Michael's hair about his face. Neither of them noticed. They galloped faster.

Even at such high speed their riding was crisp and controlled. Callie's own riding was sloppy in comparison. She was only a beginner; Michael looked as if he'd been riding all his life. More than anything, Callie wanted to ride like that.

Star and Michael raced through scrubby yellow grass, past towering saguaro and clusters of fuzzy cholla. The ground sloped upward more and more steeply; the sandy dirt gave way to rock as they approached the mountains. Like Callie and Star earlier, they lost track of how long they rode. They ran for the joy of running. Callie felt as though she ran with them, though at the same time she knew she was somewhere completely outside the dream, no more than an observer.

By the time Star and Michael turned toward home, the sun was low in the sky, and the heat wasn't as fierce as before. Near the house, Michael slowed Star to a walk. Star's mane was blown in every direction. Michael's tan face was tinted red by wind and sun. He looked happy, much happier than he had while pounding in the fence posts.

Beside Star's stall a woman waited for them. She had sun-bleached brown hair, very straight, pulled sharply back from her face. Her blue eyes were angry and tired at the same time.

"Where have you been?" Her voice sounded gravelly, older than Callie expected. "I came home expecting a fence, not just a few posts hammered into the ground!"

"I-it was too hot," Michael stammered. "I was waiting until the sun set...." The happiness drained from his face.

"You were off riding that horse of yours!"

"Star's not just any horse, Ma. She's smarter. Riding her is different from riding the others. I was thinking maybe I could race her, or ride her in the rodeo—"

"Can you fix fences with her? Can you rope a cow and bring her in for branding?"

"Of course I can. But I could do other things, too. I just need the time to train her!"

Michael's mother shook her head wearily. "Other things won't make this ranch turn a profit next year, Michael. There's another fence down on the northeast side. After you've finished stringing this one, go out and take care of that one, too. And don't come back until you've fixed it."

Michael stared at the ground. "Yes, Ma." He and Star turned back to the fields.

"Not on that horse. I'll still be waiting for the fence three days from now if you go out with her. Take your grandfather's gelding instead."

Michael sighed. He led Star back to her stall, quickly removed her saddle, and brushed her down. Then he went to get his grandfather's horse, a tired, dusty animal that always plodded along at a slow walk.

Behind him, Michael's mother muttered, "You're a good kid, Michael. If only you'd pay attention and do what you were told . . ." Her voice trailed off.

Star watched Michael saddle up the other horse and leave, staring after him until boy and horse were no more than a speck against the pale horizon.

When Callie woke, full sunlight streamed through her bedroom window. She heard her family moving around in the rest of the house. For a moment they seemed less real than the dream that had just ended.

Michael's mother didn't listen to him. His grandfather, in the other dream, hadn't listened, either. Just like Callie's family never listened. Callie sighed.

She swung herself out of bed. The insides of her legs still hurt, worse than before. Her butt was sore, too. She wondered how long she'd actually ridden the night before.

She wondered what time it was. She looked at the boxes around her. It was time to unpack, if nothing else.

First she took a shower. The cool water felt good on her sore muscles. She found clean shorts and a T-shirt in one of the boxes and put them on.

Mom and Dad were in the living room, hanging pale blue curtains over the windows. Melissa was in her bedroom, taping pictures of guys from magazines to the walls. Callie retreated back into her own room and started opening boxes.

She made her bed, loaded her clothes into drawers, threw a pile of stuffed animals onto her bed. Melissa thought Callie was childish for keeping her stuffed animals, but Callie had owned some of them all her life. She wasn't about to throw them away now.

When she reached the box with her clock radio, she walked into the living room and asked, "What time is it?"

Holding a hammer in one hand and the end of a curtain rod in the other, Mom glanced at her watch. "Two-fifteen."

Callie had known it was late, but not that late. Then again, she hadn't gone to sleep until nearly morning.

"Did you really just wake up?" Mom asked. "You look tired. Are you feeling okay?" She dropped the hammer onto the couch and used her free hand to feel Callie's forehead.

"I'm fine," Callie said.

"Maybe it's the heat," Mom said. "Even with the air-conditioning running all the time, I find I'm having a hard time getting used to it. Your friends Josh and Amy warned me that it's easy to get dehydrated here. Why don't you get something to drink?"

Callie nodded and went into the kitchen. Behind her, she heard Mom hammering nails into the wall. She poured herself a large glass of juice and took it into her room. She set the clock to the right time, then continued opening boxes. As she unpacked she kept glancing at the window, hoping to catch a flash of gray mane or tail.

Even if Star appeared right then, Callie couldn't ride her, though. She had to wait until everyone else went to sleep. Night was still hours away.

Callie set her book of horse pictures down on the dresser, right on top of a book of unicorn paintings. She kicked the box the books had come from into a corner. She was tired of unpacking. She decided to go outside instead.

The air outside was hot, as always. Callie almost turned around and went right back in again, but then she saw Amy sitting in front of her house. Amy held a book in one hand; her eyes were intent on it. A half-empty glass of water sat on the ground beside her. Callie crossed the street and walked over to her.

Amy was absorbed in her reading; she didn't notice Callie right away. Callie stood in front of her, shifting awkwardly from one foot to the other, wondering if she should say something. She looked at the cover of Amy's book. There was a saguaro on the cover, and also a coyote. It seemed to be some sort of adventure set in the Old West. Tucson, Callie realized, had once been the Old West. Probably back when her house had been a ranch. How strange.

Amy finally looked up. "Oh, hi." She set the book down beside her and stood.

"Good book?" Callie asked.

Amy shrugged. "It's okay." She reached for her water, took a long sip, and set it down again. "So," she said with a grin, "when do you want to go riding again? Josh says the stables are still pretty quiet."

"I can't," Callie said. "Mom and Dad won't let me." She could sneak rides on Star, but she couldn't sneak rides at the stables.

Amy looked puzzled. "Why not?"

Callie sighed. "They think it's too dangerous."

Amy squinted. "Dangerous?" She ran a hand through her limp hair. "Riding a horse is safer than driving a car, you know."

"Tell that to Melissa."

"Is your sister scared of everything?" Amy's voice was sharp.

"Yeah. I guess she is." Callie hadn't thought about Melissa that way before.

"One of these days she'll get in trouble for it.

What's she going to do when something really frightening happens?"

"She's done fine so far," Callie said. Then again, had anything truly frightening ever happened to Melissa—or to Callie, for that matter? The worst thing in Callie's life till now had been moving across the country.

Callie glanced at Amy. Compared to having your parents die, moving wasn't very frightening at all.

Amy shrugged. "Well, if your parents ever change their minds, let me know. Josh would be happy to take you out again. He says you're pretty good with horses, and he thinks Melissa could learn, if she stopped panicking first."

"Thanks," Callie said. She wanted to tell Amy about riding Star. Amy would understand why the horse was so wonderful. But Callie remembered how Amy hadn't even noticed Star. She couldn't tell Amy about the horse, any more than she could tell her own family. The secret had to stay between Callie and Star. In a way, Callie liked having a secret. It made her feel special somehow.

So long as the secret stayed hidden, even Melissa couldn't take that feeling away from her.

Chapter Nine

Callie ate dinner quickly that night. Mom had cooked fried chicken, which Callie liked, but she barely tasted it. All she could think about was going back to her room. Whenever Star returned, Callie didn't want to miss her. She left the table as soon as possible, slammed her bedroom door shut behind her, changed into jeans (she wasn't sure she could ride in shorts), and crouched by the window, waiting. She knew she couldn't actually ride until after everyone went to bed, but she still wanted to be there whenever Star appeared. Maybe she could even figure out where the horse came from.

She waited a long time. For a while she lay in bed and restlessly flipped through her book of horse pictures, but that only made her want to ride Star more badly. After what seemed like hours, she heard Melissa go into her room. Even later, Dad called, "Lights out, Callie! It's time for bed."

Callie turned off her light, but she didn't go to bed. She stayed by the window. She fell asleep sitting there, worrying that Star might not show up this time.

As soon as she fell asleep she dreamed. This time Callie wasn't surprised when she saw Michael riding Star. She found herself more and more curious about him. Who was he, anyway? Why did she keep dreaming about him?

In the dream, it was daytime; the sun shone brightly overhead. Michael was more somber than in the other two dreams. His eyes were rimmed with red, as though he'd been crying. Star felt his sadness. She moved slowly, with less fire in her steps than usual.

They walked to the gully, as before, but this time they didn't cross it. Instead they turned and followed the sandy depression away from the house, into fields Callie hadn't seen before. They walked up to a small enclosure surrounded by an uneven wooden fence. Michael dismounted, tied Star's reins to the fence, and stepped into the enclosure. Star stood where Michael left her, watching him.

Some small flat stones were stuck into the ground. Michael walked past them to a larger stone. Words were etched on that stone, but Callie couldn't make out the writing. Michael knelt in front of the stone. If the rocks on the ground cut into his jean-clad legs or the hot sand burned his palms, he didn't seem to notice—or care.

"Dad," he said, bowing his head. He was quiet for a long time. A tear ran down his face. He brushed it angrily away, smearing dirt across his cheek. "Two years," he whispered, so low Callie could barely hear. "I can't believe you've been gone for two years. I miss you so much."

Callie realized that the stone was a gravestone, that Michael knelt by his father's grave. Her stomach tightened. She remembered Amy explaining how her own parents had died.

Star stretched her neck over the fence, nudging Michael's shoulder with her nose. Michael smiled at her warm breath on his neck. He stood, then turned and threw his arms around Star. Star stood perfectly still, letting Michael cry into her mane. Horses couldn't cry, but Callie knew Star was sad, too.

After a long time Michael mounted the horse again. Together they rode away from the graveyard, toward mountains that shimmered with heat. Star sped into a gallop. The wind dried the tears from Michael's face and put the fire back into Star's steps.

At one point Star slowed down. She turned her head back toward home, ears perked as if asking a question.

"No," Michael said. His voice was fierce. "I'm not going back there. Not yet. They'll yell at me later, but I don't care."

Star broke into a gallop once more. For the

rest of the long afternoon, she kept running. She understood that just then, more than anything, Michael needed to run with her.

And Star, feeling his unhappiness, needed to run as well.

Callie woke up crying. That was strange; she'd never had a dream that made her cry before. But then, she'd never had dreams she remembered so clearly, either. She wondered why these dreams were different. Michael felt so real, almost as if Callie could reach through her dreams and touch him.

Michael was just someone her dreams had made up, wasn't he? Callie had trouble believing that, though no other explanation made sense.

Star was real, though; Callie knew that much. She suddenly, desperately wanted to see the horse. As if in response, her spine started tingling.

Callie didn't need to look out the window. She knew Star was there. She pulled on her sneakers and ran from her room. The house was dark; everyone was asleep. She ran through the kitchen, pulling the door open and then throwing it shut behind her. It slammed loudly, and she cringed. She hoped no one had heard.

She raced around back. Star stood in the

yard, just as Callie knew she would. All at once, Callie didn't feel like crying at all. She ran to Star. Star stood very still, staring at Callie with dark, calm eyes. Through those eyes, Callie thought she felt something: a touch of the same sadness she'd felt in her dream.

Callie swung onto Star's back more easily this time; she was beginning to get used to it. She sat in the saddle, waiting for her eyes to adjust to the dark. The moon had shrunk to half-size, but it still cast faint light throughout the yard.

Had Star really read Callie's thoughts the night before? Or had Callie imagined it?

Walk, Callie thought.

Star walked.

Trot. Canter. Gallop.

Star burst into a four-beat run. The fiery gait took Callie's breath away. She laughed with joy. She felt as though she and Star were flying together.

Star raced to the gully, then slowed back down to a walk. She leaned down and sniffed the ground, and she stepped down into the depression. She began to follow the sandy dirt toward the edge of their land.

Ice trickled down Callie's spine. Star was following the same route Michael had taken in her dream.

"Stop," Callie whispered. "Please." The fact

that Star chose that night to follow the gully was probably just a coincidence. Still, she couldn't help fearing that if Star kept walking, they might find the rough graveyard where Michael had knelt.

Star stopped. She stamped her foot, but the gesture was gentle, like a shrug. Star leaned down and took a huge bite from one of the shrubs in the gully. Then she turned and walked back to the house, stopping right in front of Callie's window.

"Callie?" someone called.

Callie tensed at the sound.

"Callie, where are you?" It was Melissa, calling from the side of the house. Star's ears perked forward.

Callie couldn't let Melissa catch her riding. She quickly dismounted. She gave Star a quick hug, then hurried around the house. Melissa stood by the patio door, still calling.

"I'm here." Callie waved and walked over to Melissa. She forced herself to smile, as if there were nothing unusual about being out in the middle of the night.

Melissa put her hands on her hips, glaring. "Where were you?"

"Out back," Callie said.

"I looked out back."

Callie shrugged. "It's dark. Maybe you just didn't see me." She didn't know how Melissa could have missed her, but she was grateful. That meant Melissa hadn't seen Star, either.

Melissa narrowed her eyes. "Where were you really, Callie? Do Mom and Dad know you've been sneaking out at night? I'm amazed they didn't hear you run out; but then the AC is pretty loud."

"This is the first time," Callie lied. "I couldn't sleep. I just wanted some air."

Melissa stared at Callie, and Callie knew her sister didn't believe her. She remembered that Melissa had found her outside two nights earlier.

Behind her, Callie caught the sound of hooves against the dirt. She heard a horse snort softly.

No, Callie thought desperately to Star. *Don't follow me. Stay out back.*

Star either didn't understand that thought or decided to ignore it. She stepped around the house, leaning her head heavily on Callie's shoulder. Her nose was wet against Callie's neck.

Callie pushed Star away. "Go home," she whispered, though she had no idea where Star's real home was. "Go on."

Melissa's expression turned strange. "Who are you talking to?"

Callie swallowed. "Just some horse," she blurted. "I've never seen her before. I don't know where she came from."

Melissa shook her head. "There's no horse here, Callie. Stop being weird. Is this some sort of little kid's game?"

Callie's cheeks turned red. "It's not a game! And I'm not a little kid!"

"You have a strange way of showing it. One trail ride and you're imagining ponies."

"I'm not imagining anything!" Callie pulled back a fist and swung at her sister. Melissa ducked. Callie's hand swished through empty air. Callie pulled back her hand again, then stopped. She didn't really want to hit Melissa. She didn't want to fight at all. She just wanted to get away.

She could get away. As far away as she wanted. Just like Michael.

Callie turned back to Star. She mounted the horse, swinging into the saddle more smoothly than ever.

"Callie!" Melissa screeched. Her jaw fell open. The color drained from her face. Even in the moonlight, Callie saw how pale she was. "Callie, where are you?"

Why did Melissa keep acting as though she didn't see anything? "I'm right here," Callie said.

Melissa didn't seem to hear her. She kept staring straight ahead. Callie waved her hands in front of Melissa's face. She stuck her tongue out at her. Melissa didn't even blink.

Melissa couldn't see Callie and Star.

Amy hadn't seen Star, either. Callie started trembling. The horse was really invisible to them. And when Callie rode, she was invisible, too. That was impossible; she knew it was. Yet Melissa stood there, looking around wildly now, with no idea that Callie sat right in front of her.

Star swung her head around to look at Callie. Callie stared back at the horse. Slowly she stopped shaking. Being invisible wasn't frightening, not when she stopped to think about it. It was just startling.

"You're magic," Callie whispered. "Aren't you?" A horse like this could probably choose any rider in the world, yet she came back to Callie, night after night. Callie could hardly believe it.

Joy bubbled up in Callie, so strong she thought she'd burst. Star snorted, as if laughing with her. Melissa still didn't hear. Callie laughed out loud. Not only had she found a magic horse; she'd also found a way that Melissa couldn't bother her.

Callie and Star turned away from Melissa and walked back into the yard, to the corral. Melissa didn't follow.

Callie and Star rode together beneath the waning moon. Callie felt her love for the horse growing stronger and stronger. She felt Star's love for her growing, too, though she couldn't explain how.

They rode until dawn lit the sky. Melissa didn't call out to Callie again. No one came to make Callie stop riding or to take Star away.

As long as Callie was invisible, no one could tell her what to do.

Callie expected Melissa to wake their parents, but she hadn't. When Callie stepped back inside, the house was silent. She tiptoed down the hall. A light shone beneath Melissa's closed door, but Mom and Dad's room was dark. Callie slipped quietly into her own room.

Why hadn't Melissa said anything to them? Callie knew better than to think her sister cared about keeping Callie's secret. Maybe Melissa didn't think Mom and Dad would believe her. That made sense. Callie herself barely believed she'd been invisible. If not for Melissa's reaction, Callie still might not know about Star's magic.

Callie kicked off her shoes, changed into pajamas, and climbed into bed. She fell asleep dreaming of invisible rides through dark, windy fields. For once, Michael didn't appear at all.

Chapter Ten

In a small corner of her mind, Callie still feared Star wouldn't come back again. She couldn't believe that a magical horse would want to return to her every night. Star did return that night, though. She came back the next night, too, and the night after that. Slowly Callie stopped wondering whether the horse would appear and started expecting her to. And somehow each ride with Star felt more magical than the last.

Callie's riding improved. She felt her muscles grow stronger, until her legs weren't sore anymore, no matter how long she rode. She felt more and more in control during her rides, but she didn't feel as if she was ordering Star around. Instead she felt as though she was a part of Star's fiery, graceful movement, contributing to it as much as the horse did.

Now that Callie knew Star was magical, she stopped worrying about her owners. No one could own a magic horse. Or maybe magic horses chose their owners. Maybe Star had chosen Callie. Why else would she return night after night?

At the end of each night, as the sun rose, Callie reluctantly left Star and went to sleep. After a couple of days Mom and Dad started work, so they didn't see how late she slept during the week. So long as Callie did her chores—cleaning the bathroom, emptying the trash, or unloading the dishwasher, depending on the day—they didn't seem to care.

By the time Mom and Dad got home from work, Callie had only a few hours until they slept again. That was fine with her. She was tired of trying to talk to them, tired of trying to make them listen to her. Seeing them as little as possible was much easier.

On weekends her parents wanted to explore Tucson, so Callie had to get up earlier. Mom and Dad took the girls on winding drives through the mountains, on tours of museums downtown (where the city's few tall buildings were), even once to a planetarium. Callie did her best to act interested, or at least to hide how tired she felt.

Melissa stopped talking to Callie entirely. She did look at her sister strangely sometimes, but Callie didn't care. Melissa didn't say anything to Mom and Dad about Callie's "disappearance"; that was the important thing.

Some of the time Callie was awake she spent

talking with Amy, when Amy wasn't down at Sonoran Stables riding. Amy invited Callie to ride with her a few times, but Callie always had to refuse. Knowing she could still ride Star made refusing less painful.

After a couple of weeks, riding Star was all that really mattered to her. Being with Star was enough to make Callie happy. For the first time since moving to Tucson, her life was nearly perfect.

In her dreams, however, Michael seemed more and more unhappy.

Callie dreamed about Star and Michael every night, sometimes before she rode, sometimes after. When she woke up, she felt as if she'd really been with them. Sometimes she was almost disappointed when the dreams ended; she wanted to know what happened next.

In the dreams, Star was one of many horses Michael's family owned. She was Michael's horse; she had been ever since his parents had realized she wasn't going to bear any foals. They decided Star might as well be put to work, and they gave her to Michael.

Michael said Star was better than an ordinary broodmare. He said she was more talented than any horse he'd ridden before. He wanted to train her as a rodeo horse, but his mother and grandfather wouldn't let him. They said training a horse to do anything more than work on the ranch was a waste of time. They wanted Michael to start taking on his father's responsibilities. They couldn't afford for him not to. They'd pulled him out of school so that he could spend more time working on the ranch.

Since before the war, the ranch had lost money. (The war meant World War II, Callie eventually realized; that was when she knew for sure that the dreams were set in the past.) Michael's father had died in that war, on the shores of an ocean Michael had never even seen. When he'd died, money had gotten even tighter.

To make matters worse, the summer was brutally dry. The green bushes turned brown; the grass withered away. The cattle grew thin. Michael's grandfather feared they'd have to sell some of the property to pay off their debts; Michael's mother insisted that the ranch would fall apart if they broke up the land.

Michael didn't want the ranch to fall apart, but he did want to ride Star more than they let him. Like Callie, he snuck away with the horse whenever he could. He and Star rode farther and farther from home, following old cattle trails into the mountains.

His mother and grandfather yelled whenever they caught him riding. The more Michael tried to talk to his family, the less they listened to him. At one point his mother even threatened to sell Star. Michael told Star he couldn't bear the thought of that happening. He wasn't sure what he would do if it did.

Callie felt bad for him. She was glad she didn't talk much to her family anymore.

With Star at least, she didn't have to use words.

Callie stared at the boiled cabbage on her plate, trying to convince herself to take another bite. She was too tired to eat. It was Saturday, and her parents had woken her up at seven to visit a place called the Desert Museum. The plants and animals there were interesting enough, but between the heat and the fact that Callie hadn't gone to bed until dawn, she hadn't really been able to focus on anything. Just like she couldn't focus on her plate anymore; the dish blurred in front of her.

"Callie?" Mom said. "Are you all right?"

Callie blinked. Her eyes had closed, and somehow she hadn't noticed. How long had she sat asleep in her chair, fork still raised over her dish? Everyone was looking at her.

"I'm fine," Callie said.

Mom didn't look convinced. She reached across the table and put a hand on Callie's forehead. "You don't seem to have a fever," she said, but she sounded worried.

"Aren't you feeling well?" Dad asked.

Callie tensed. "I'm fine," she said. Melissa looked at her suspiciously but didn't say anything.

"Your eyes are awfully red," Dad said. "I think we'd better take you in to the doctor, just to be safe. You'll need a physical before you start school in the fall, anyway."

"In the meantime, why don't you get some rest?" Mom said.

That meant Callie didn't have to finish dinner. She left the table before Mom could change her mind.

Behind her, Mom and Dad talked in quiet, concerned voices. Callie bit her lip. She didn't want them to worry. If they worried, they might start paying more attention to her. They might find out about Star after all.

Chapter Eleven

Callie went into her room and closed the door. Evening light streamed through the window; Mom and Dad wouldn't go to bed for hours. Callie couldn't even think about riding yet. She yawned. Her eyes were gritty and tired.

Maybe she should get some sleep. Time would pass faster that way. Now that she was in her room, though, she felt restless.

She paced the room, looking around as she did. She'd unpacked all of her own boxes, but the bottom of the closet was still filled with the boxes and trunk that Mrs. Hansen had left behind. Mom had finally called Mrs. Hansen directly, and she'd promised to send someone by as soon as possible. Mom had told Callie she'd bring the boxes into the garage this weekend if no one came; Dad said they should just throw them all away.

What was in the boxes, anyway? Whatever it was, Mrs. Hansen didn't seem to care about it very much.

Callie glanced at the window. The sky was

still pink, fading to pale blue; the first stars hadn't appeared yet. She pulled a cardboard box from the closet and sat down beside it.

The box was taped shut; she pulled the tape away. The box tore open, letting out a cloud of dust. Callie fanned the dust away, then looked inside.

She saw a battered jumble of photos. They were all black-and-white, or tinged brown the way old pictures sometimes were. She removed them one at a time, piling them beside the box. The photos were all different sizes; many were torn or bent. The edges crumbled in her hands.

The first few pictures showed an older version of Callie's house. There weren't any other houses beside it, just a few small adobe shacks. One picture showed some chickens pecking in the yard.

She dug deeper into the box. She glimpsed a photo with people in it. She pulled it out.

What she saw stopped her cold.

Callie's hands shook, and the picture fell to the floor. She stared at the spot where it landed. She couldn't believe what she saw.

The picture was of Michael. His hair blew into his face, the same way it did in Callie's dreams. He squinted at the sun. He looked strange in black and white. The sky and mountains behind him looked strange, too, cast in muted shades of gray, with none of the desert's brightness.

Michael couldn't be real, even if he felt that way in Callie's dreams. This must be some other boy, one who reminded her of Michael. She was more tired than she'd realized. She reached into the box and pulled out another picture.

Michael and his mother were both in this one, standing beside a wobbly calf. In the next picture Michael's grandfather sat in a battered old car.

Callie flipped through the pictures more quickly. While Michael wasn't in all of the pictures, he was in most of them. Sometimes he stood alone, sometimes with his mother or grandfather. Sometimes he looked younger than in Callie's dreams, but never much older. In one framed picture, more formally posed than the rest, he stood beside a tall man in uniform. His father.

Callie felt cold and strange. Even the clothes Michael wore were familiar; her dreams had gotten every last detail right.

Only a few photos remained in the box. Callie dumped them onto the floor. A black-and-white snapshot tumbled away from the rest of the pile; she picked it up. The picture was fuzzier than the others, torn in half and taped back together. Callie swallowed hard.

Michael sat on a horse. A horse with a coat that shone even in black and white. A horse with dark, bottomless eyes. A horse with a white mark like a star on her forehead.

Callie had spent too much time riding Star to think she was imagining things now. She stared at the picture for a long time. The sun set, and rosy light filled her room.

Could Michael and his family have really existed once? Could Michael have lived in her house, back when it was a ranch? Could he have slept in Callie's room? Ice ran down Callie's spine. Could he have owned Star? Surely he would have taken Star with him when he left. Had Mrs. Hansen inherited Star, then abandoned her with the bedroom furniture? Callie couldn't believe that.

The picture of Star slipped from Callie's fingers and landed facedown on the floor. Something was written in pencil on the back. Callie picked the photo up again for a closer look.

Michael Hansen, the writing said.

Mrs. Hansen, the women they'd bought the house from, was Michael's mother. She was the woman in Callie's dreams who kept telling Michael to stop riding. Except that now she was much older, and she lived in a nursing home. The thought made Callie shiver.

Why would she dream about Mrs. Hansen's

son? For that matter, why hadn't Michael come to pick up his own things?

All of a sudden, Callie didn't want to think about it. She wanted to pretend she had never seen the pictures in the first place. She threw them back into the box and shoved the box across the room.

Dusk faded, leaving the room in shadow. Callie stood and flipped the light on. She wanted to run from the room. She wanted to find Star. She wished her parents—and Melissa—would hurry up and go to sleep.

Callie walked back to the closet. She ignored the other boxes piled there. They might have more pictures in them. Instead she reached under the boxes and pulled out the trunk. It was larger than most trunks, made of dented green metal. Something banged inside as Callie dragged it into the room.

She knelt beside the trunk and undid the latch. The lid resisted for a moment, then creaked open. Callie looked inside.

"No," she whispered. Her breath caught in her throat. "No, it can't be." What she saw was much worse than the pictures: a dusty old saddle.

Slowly, hands shaking, she pulled the saddle out. The leather was brittle with age, but otherwise the saddle matched Star's exactly. There were even the same black scorch marks around the edges. The smell of smoke was faint but still noticeable.

Star wore that saddle every night. Callie rode on it. Yet the saddle was covered with dust. It had been in the trunk for years. A saddle couldn't be in two places at once.

Unless one of them wasn't real.

Maybe Callie had imagined Star and Michael both. Maybe she'd seen the pictures and saddle before, then forgotten them somehow. Maybe, without realizing it, she was playing some sort of game, just like Melissa said she was. That would explain why no one else could see the horse.

Callie remembered something Amy had said. *I know what's real and what's not real, whatever some people might think.* Maybe Callie didn't know what was real. Maybe she was going crazy.

No. She took one deep breath, then another. If she'd imagined Star, she'd have imagined her differently. Star wouldn't have tried to kick Callie, and she wouldn't have run away. If Star were imaginary, she would have done exactly what Callie wanted her to, from the very first time they'd met.

Star was real, then. But she still wasn't an ordinary horse. She was invisible, and she made Callie invisible, too. She could read Callie's thoughts and sometimes her emotions. Star could calm Callie. She could make Callie feel her love.

Star had belonged to Michael before she'd belonged to Callie. The pictures made that much clear. Somehow, impossibly, Callie had dreamed about their life together. Maybe the dreams came from Star. Maybe she saw things as Star remembered them. Star could read Callie's thoughts, after all; maybe Callie could read Star's thoughts—and memories—in turn.

Something was wrong, though. It took Callie a moment to figure out what.

Michael's father had died in World War II. But that war had happened such a long time ago; only her grandparents even remembered it, and they had been kids at the time. If Star had lived all the way back then, how could she be alive now? Callie wasn't sure how long horses lived, but it couldn't be over fifty years. Star should be dead by now.

Callie had another idea, one so strange she tried to convince herself it was silly. It made sense, though. Star was invisible. Star shouldn't still be alive.

Maybe Star was a ghost.

Callie shivered at the thought. As she did she felt the familiar tingling down her spine. She looked out the window. Star stared back at her. Had the horse been watching the whole time Callie looked at the pictures and saddle?

Was Star really a ghost? She looked solid enough. Ghosts were supposed to be smoky, unreal, even a little bit scary. Star was none of those things.

Callie wanted to run out to Star, to touch her, to prove to herself that the horse was still real, the same horse she'd been riding every night.

She heard Mom, Dad, and Melissa talking in the kitchen. She couldn't ride yet; someone would notice if she was gone for too long. She needed to at least see Star, though.

Callie stood. Her left foot had fallen asleep; she shook it until the numbness went away. Then she tiptoed through the living room, closing the front door softly so that Mom and Dad wouldn't hear.

Star snorted as Callie stepped around the side of the house. The horse trotted eagerly up to her. Star's nose bumped into Callie's chest; she stopped short just in time to avoid knocking Callie over.

Star's breath felt warm and real on Callie's neck. Star's coat was silky against her cheek. If Star was a ghost, then ghosts were nothing like Callie had thought they were. She threw her arms around the horse.

If Star was a ghost, why would she appear outside Callie's window every night? Was Callie special somehow?

There was another possibility, one Callie liked less. What if Star still thought Callie's room belonged to Michael? What if she was waiting for him, not Callie, when she stood outside each night? Maybe Star didn't care about Callie at all.

Star nudged Callie with her wet nose. Callie felt the horse's love. Even if Star had at first come looking for Michael, she still loved Callie. She let Callie ride her every night. She was Callie's horse now. That was all that really mattered.

"Callie?" Dad called. She saw him walking around the house and quickly dropped her hold on Star. "Callie, why aren't you resting?" His voice sounded tired and a little bit worried.

"I was just getting some air," Callie said. Dad opened his mouth to say something, but Callie ran past him. She didn't want to talk to him. He wouldn't really hear what she had to say, anyway. She ran into her room and slammed the door.

Dad followed more slowly. Callie was afraid he'd knock on her door, but he didn't. Instead he sat down in the living room and turned on the TV.

Callie walked to the window. Star still stood there. "I'll be out to ride you soon," Callie promised.

She knelt by the window and stared at Star, waiting for everyone else to go to sleep.

Chapter Twelve

Dad watched TV longer than Callie expected. She yawned, then closed her eyes. Once or twice she shook herself awake, but finally she fell into a deeper sleep.

As always, she dreamed.

The dream began like any other. Michael's grandfather was yelling about a water trough Michael had forgotten to fill the night before. With the summer so dry, the only water the cattle got was what Michael and his family gave them. Michael's grandfather told Michael to go out and fill the trough right away and to check on the other troughs, too. The last thing they needed was for the cattle to die of dehydration.

"I hate him," Michael muttered as he saddled Star. "I hate them both. They don't understand anything but this stupid old ranch. Let them find someone else to take care of it. I want to go far away. You'd come with me, wouldn't you, Star?"

Star perked her ears forward, as if intrigued by the idea.

"Michael!" His grandfather's voice cut through the morning.

"I'm going!" Michael said. He mounted Star and whirled away from his grandfather, galloping fast and hard.

He rode toward the trough until he was out of his grandfather's sight. Then he turned abruptly toward the mountains instead. "I'll worry about the trough later," he told Star. His voice was fierce; Callie had never seen him quite so angry. "They haven't let me ride you in days," he said, scowling. "And Mom's talking again about selling you. Who knows how much time we have left?"

They galloped through fields of dead grass and over dry, hard soil. There still hadn't been rain, not through all the long, hot summer.

Above them, the sky was blue, the sun bright and hot. Over the Catalinas, however, clouds were gathering, billows of gray piling up on one another.

The fields grew steeper and rockier as they approached the mountains. Star kept running, barely slowing down to pick her way among the rocks. She turned onto an old trail that led steeply upward. There was more rock than soil there, yet cacti and trees grew thick around the trail. Star had to slow down after all, first to a trot, then to a walk. She and Michael rode farther from home than they ever had before.

Rock walls rose on either side of them. The walls grew steeper, until all of a sudden they were in a canyon. Star grew more nervous and twitchy the farther in they walked, but she didn't stop.

All of a sudden there was a low rumble overhead. Michael brought Star to a halt and looked up. Though the sun still shone brightly to the left, dark clouds were directly above them. Callie had never seen anything like those clouds before. They were black as coal, yet the sun lit them underneath, making them glitter as though they had diamonds hidden inside.

Another rumble. Star nickered and backed nervously downhill. Her whole body twitched. A bolt of lightning struck out from beneath the clouds. The air around Star and Michael sizzled.

Michael's face went white. "Let's go home," he whispered.

Star didn't need any encouragement. She nickered again, a frightened sound that echoed like a warning through the canyon. Then she whirled around and took off downhill as fast as she could. She raced over the uneven rocks, her gait somewhere between a trot and a canter, rough enough that Michael was jostled about in the saddle. Lightning struck again and again. The clouds no longer glistened; they looked dark and bruised.

"We have to get out of here!" Michael yelled.

The canyon seemed much longer riding out than riding in.

There was another flash of light, and then a sickening burnt smell. The dead grass in front of Star and Michael exploded into flames.

Star whirled around again, feet slipping wildly on the rocks. The smell of burning grass and cacti filled her nostrils, turning her fear to raw terror. Smoke was everywhere; so was the crackle of burning grass. She couldn't think. All she could do was run.

A flicker of flame touched Star's tail. Hair burned away; the skin below blistered. Star leaped forward, desperate to escape the heat. Michael grabbed Star's mane, struggling to hold on, but Star knew only the stench of her own burning hair. The crackling behind her grew louder. She reared up to jump again. Michael slid from her back. He hit the rocks headfirst with a sickening crack.

Star didn't look back. She ran deeper into the canyon, flames at her heels. She was aware of nothing but the suffocating smoke and the need to escape the flames.

The dream cut off abruptly. Callie woke up screaming.

Chapter Thirteen

Someone shook her. Callie didn't know who. She didn't care. She only saw Star, running through the fire.

"Callie, wake up!" Dad gripped her shoulders and shook her harder.

She'd fallen asleep by the window again; the floor was hard against her knees. She bolted to her feet, looking wildly around the room, like a scared animal. She gulped deep breaths of air, wanting only to erase the memory of smoke and burning hair.

"Callie, what is it?" Dad's face was tight and worried. Mom and Melissa stood in the room, too, by the door, staring at her.

Callie didn't care about them. She cared only about Star; she needed to know the horse was all right. She pulled fiercely away from Dad and ran from the room, past Mom and Melissa, through the house and into the yard. Star was there. Callie drew in a relieved breath, tasting the dusty, dry scent of the desert. The horse was slick with sweat; her wet coat glistened beneath the full moon. Callie threw her arms around the horse's neck. Star trembled; Callie felt the horse's raw fear. She held Star tighter.

"Did you die like that?" Callie began to cry. "In the flames?"

As soon as Callie asked, she knew that wasn't how it happened. Not quite. In a brief flash—almost like one of her dreams, except that she was wide awake now—Callie saw the rest of the story: Star escaping the canyon and running all the way home; Michael's mother in tears, wandering numbly around Michael's room, unable even to think about moving his things; his grandfather saying, sadly, "There's no reason not to sell off the land now"; Star weakened from her burns, but dying of something else—her guilt at abandoning Michael. Callie hadn't known horses could feel guilt, but Star felt it as strongly as any human.

"Callie!" She heard her family running across the yard. She couldn't face them. They'd ask her what had happened. If she told them, they'd make her give up Star. She couldn't do that, not now.

She didn't have to. She jumped onto Star's back.

The moment she did, Star broke into a gallop. Callie screamed. It was the fastest, roughest gallop she'd ever felt. Behind her, Melissa was yelling, demanding to know where Callie had disappeared to. Callie didn't care. She clutched at the saddle, fighting to stay seated.

She tried to slow Star down. *Canter*, she thought. *Trot. Walk.* For the first time, Star ignored her.

When they reached the dry wash, Star turned to follow it, running even faster. Callie pulled back on the reins. Star kept going. The backs of houses flew by on either side of them.

"Stop!" Callie yelled. "Please stop!" The horse didn't even seem to know that Callie was there. Callie's yells turned into choking sobs.

The wash branched. Star didn't hesitate; she took the branch that led toward the mountains. Around them, the houses thinned. Once a narrow bridge crossed the gully; Callie ducked just in time to keep from hitting her head.

She stopped yelling. She took one deep breath, then another. She couldn't calm Star if she panicked herself. Melissa had panicked on their trail ride, and that had only gotten her into more trouble.

Callie loosened her grip on the saddle. She sat up straighter, finding her balance. Her throat was dry, and her hands ached from holding on so tightly. She tried to match her breathing to the rhythm of Star's running. She looked ahead, trying to figure out where Star was going.

Star galloped past the last houses and into the foothills of the mountains. An old trail branched away from the wash. Star took it, barely slowing as she turned. Rocks slid out from beneath the horse's feet, but she kept running. The ground turned rougher, but Star slowed only slightly. Rock walls rose on both sides of them.

Then, all of a sudden, Star stopped short. Callie flew forward; she grabbed the saddle horn to keep from falling. She dismounted quickly, before Star could run again. She lifted Star's reins over her head, holding them tightly. Maybe she could lead Star back home.

Star was breathing hard. Her coat foamed with sweat. Callie stared at the horse. "What's wrong with you?" she asked. Running like that didn't make any sense, no matter how scared or upset Star was.

Callie tugged gently on Star's reins, trying to lead the horse back downhill. She managed to turn Star around, so that she was facing the right direction, but after that, Star wouldn't budge. She stood still as stone, no matter how hard Callie pulled on the reins.

Callie sighed. She looked around, trying to guess how far she was from home. Beneath the full moon, she saw the mountains perfectly. Canyon walls towered on either side of her. Rocks and dry grass lay scattered at her feet.

Callie caught her breath. She knew exactly where they were: the same place as in her last dream.

"This is where it happened, isn't it?" Callie dropped the reins and hugged Star tightly. She buried her head against the horse's neck, smelling sweat and fear.

Callie also smelled something else. Smoke, coming from behind her.

Star nickered; the sound echoed through the canyon. She jerked free of Callie and backed uphill. Callie's feet were frozen to the ground. She could only watch numbly as Star stepped out of her reach. The horse's ears went back. Her tail swished fitfully from side to side. She had the same nervous look she'd had when she first ran from Callie, what seemed like ages before, only now her eyes were wild, large with terror.

The smell of smoke grew stronger. Callie was afraid to turn around. Behind her, she heard the crackling of dry brush, just like in her dream. *This can't really be happening*, she thought, but the crackling grew louder. Her stomach twisted into a painful knot. The dream was happening all over again, only this time she was the one trapped in the canyon.

Somehow she and Star had to get out of there. Callie forced her feet from where she stood and stepped forward. Star stopped backing away and stared at her, trembling. Callie wanted to move faster, but she knew that if she did, Star would run away. Instead Callie approached slowly, pausing after each step.

One more step, and Star's reins would be within Callie's reach. One more step—

Callie tripped over something. She looked down and saw a boy sprawled facedown on the rocks. He wasn't moving, but Callie heard his raspy breathing.

Callie knelt by his side. Whoever he was, she couldn't just leave him there. Behind her, she heard the crash of hooves against stones. Star had run after all. Just like she'd run when she first met Callie. Just like she'd run from Michael during the other fire. She'd left Callie in the canyon, alone.

Or maybe not completely alone. Callie shook the boy. He didn't stir. She turned him over.

Callie caught her breath. She knew who this was. She should have known from the moment she first saw him lying there. Dark hair fell into his face; Callie brushed it away and looked at him. "So you're Michael," she whispered.

Callie didn't know what he was doing there, but she didn't have time to worry about that. She had to get both of them out of the mountains. She saw the smoke now, hanging like haze in the air around her. The crackling sound was closer, too.

She lifted Michael from the ground and tried

to carry him. He was too heavy; after a couple of steps she stumbled. She had to set him down again.

Panic caught at the back of Callie's throat; fear trickled down her spine. She looked wildly around. If she found Star, maybe she could somehow get Michael onto the horse's back. With Star's help, maybe all three of them could get out of the mountains.

"Star!" Callie yelled. "Star, where are you?" Callie felt heat at her back. She took a few steps up the canyon. Star was nowhere in sight. Callie thought, with all her strength, *Star, come here. I need you.*

Callie felt something—a frightened flicker at a corner of her mind.

Star? The smoke was thicker now. Dark clouds of it rolled through the air around Callie, clogging her throat and making her eyes tear.

Callie heard Star's slow steps. She looked up the canyon and saw the horse step out from behind a cluster of trees and then stop, just a few yards beyond Callie's reach. Star's eyes were still wild. Her mane was tangled and matted with sweat. One wrong move and she would run again.

Callie fought her own fear. She fought to make her thoughts calmer than they'd ever been. She shut out the crackling and the smoke. She shut out everything but Star's dark eyes.

When Callie had arrived in the desert, Star had calmed her. The horse had made her less miserable in the strange new place she had to live. Now it was Callie's turn to calm Star.

"It's okay, girl. It's okay." Callie walked toward Star, slowly, her eyes never leaving the horse. The frightened presence in Callie's mind settled down.

Star lifted a hoof and tentatively stepped forward. She walked the last few steps to Callie on her own. Callie took the reins. She held them more tightly than she'd ever held anything.

Callie led Star to Michael. She could barely see through the smoke now. Out of the corner of her eye, she glimpsed a flicker of flame. She coughed from the smoke, but she didn't stop walking.

When Callie dropped the reins, Star stood very still. Callie lifted Michael from the ground. She staggered under his weight, and she nearly dropped him. But instead she gritted her teeth, and she half lifted, half threw Michael over the saddle.

"Let's go home," Callie whispered.

Star just stared at her. Callie still felt the horse's fear, but also her love—and her trust.

Callie lifted the reins over Star's head. She

reached one foot toward the stirrups to mount behind Michael.

She heard a strange roaring sound behind her. She felt a blast of heat. The canyon exploded in flames. Heat surrounded her; she felt pain like she'd never felt before.

Callie fell, screaming as she dropped through the fire.

Chapter Fourteen

As suddenly as it had started, the fire stopped. Callie hit cool, hard rocks. Pain shot through her head. For a long time she just lay on the ground, trying to believe she was still alive. She touched one arm, and her skin was cool. Ghost flames, she thought dazedly. The fire hadn't been real. Or rather, it had been once, but that was a long time ago.

Callie opened her eyes. The moon had nearly set; only faint silver-blue light lit the canyon. Above her the sky was filled with dizzying stars. The air smelled dry and dusty. A bird trilled thinly through the air, paused as if waiting for an answer, then trilled again. Farther away, something howled and was silent. There was no sign the mountain had ever burned at all.

"Star!" a boy's voice cried. "You came back!"

Callie sat up. Her head rang, and for a moment the world spun crazily around her; then everything was still.

Michael stood just a few feet away from Callie, his arms around Star's neck. He buried his face against Star's shoulder and choked on a sob. "You came back," he whispered. "I knew you would." Star turned her head to nuzzle Michael's neck.

Tears trickled down Callie's cheeks. Star had returned to Michael. That was the reason the horse had bolted into the mountains in the first place—to face the danger she'd once run from, to make up for abandoning Michael. Callie should be happy for the horse—for both of them.

But now that Star had found Michael, where did that leave Callie?

Star was Michael's horse. Even though Callie had ridden Star every night, even though Callie was the one who had helped her face the flames, Star didn't belong to Callie.

Callie felt anger rise in her. "It isn't fair!" she yelled. "You shouldn't have come in the first place if you weren't going to stay!"

Star snorted. She lifted her head, stepping sideways away from Michael. Michael watched Star, but he didn't seem to notice Callie at all. He looked straight through her. Maybe to Michael, Callie was the ghost.

Star stared at Callie. In the fading moonlight, the mark on her forehead glowed.

Callie felt the horse's love for her, as real and solid as anything she'd ever felt. Star cared for Callie as much as Callie cared for Star. The fact that Star didn't belong to Callie didn't change that.

Callie brushed her tears away. She ran up to Star and wrapped her arms around the horse.

Callie held Star for a long time, breathing the sweet smell of her mane, listening to her breath move softly in and out. She wanted to hold Star forever, to stop her from leaving.

She didn't, though. With a sigh she stepped back, letting Star go.

Star returned to Michael's side. He mounted without a sound.

"Good-bye," Callie said.

Star snorted, but Michael didn't answer her. He still didn't see Callie. He didn't know—or care—what she'd done for him. All of a sudden that made Callie angry.

"You could say something!" Callie felt a fresh round of tears coming, and she sniffled to fight them. "You could at least thank me!" Callie took a deep breath, preparing to yell some more.

Then she stopped herself. Michael was stroking Star's mane and staring straight ahead. He couldn't see her. Probably he couldn't hear what she said.

That wasn't fair, either.

But lots of things weren't fair. If Michael couldn't hear her, nothing would change that.

She might as well save her complaining for things she could do something about.

"Good-bye," Callie whispered. The words sounded loud in the still night. "I'll miss you."

Star nodded once, so seriously and respectfully that Callie cried again after all. Then Star and Michael rode away together. Callie watched them walk down the canyon. As they shrank with distance, they also grew paler, flickering like the stars that shone above them. For just a moment Callie saw through them to the canyon walls. Another moment and they were gone.

Callie stood alone in the canyon.

The moon had completely disappeared now, and even the stars were beginning to fade. She turned around and saw the pale orange glow of dawn. The light slowly spread over the mountains, turning gray to gold. She took a deep breath, inhaling the scent of some sweet desert plant. Even with Star gone, the mountains and the desert were still beautiful. She wondered how she'd ever thought otherwise.

It was time to go home. Callie looked down the canyon; already the sun was above the rocky walls.

She'd ridden into the canyon on horseback. She wondered how long it would take to walk out on foot.

*   *   *

It took much longer than Callie expected. She'd hoped to walk all the way home, but by the time she reached the first houses, the sun was high. The day was hot, and Callie was thirsty. Her feet burned in her sneakers. The ringing in her head had turned into a headache.

She knocked on a door and asked if she could call her parents. She must have looked more tired than she thought. The woman who answered let her right in and gave her a large glass of iced tea, too.

Dad answered the phone. His voice sounded tired, as if he'd been up all night, but relieved as well. He asked her if she was all right, then he asked her where she was. Callie didn't know how to get there by car; the woman had to give Dad directions.

The house must have been much closer by car than the way Callie and Star had gone; Mom, Dad, and Melissa arrived fifteen minutes later. All three of them looked tired. Later Callie would find out that Mom and Dad had been out searching most of the night; they'd only just come in when she'd called.

Mom and Dad were both crying. Melissa's eyes were rimmed with red, as if she'd been crying, too. That surprised Callie; she'd almost thought her sister would be glad to get rid of her.

Callie had planned to tell her parents what had

happened; she couldn't think of any other way to explain where she'd been. But when she saw how upset they were, she couldn't do it. Telling them about ghost horses and ghost fires would only scare them more. Or maybe they wouldn't believe Callie at all. She wasn't sure which would be worse.

Instead she told them she'd run away. That was the sort of thing parents could cope with, right?

Not according to Dad. "What did you think you were doing?" he demanded as Mom drove home. His worry had been replaced by anger. "Don't you know how dangerous it is to be out alone at night? You could have been killed—or worse!"

"Dad—" Callie tried to cut in, but he kept yelling. He wouldn't listen to Callie. He was just like Michael's parents. Callie wanted to yell back.

Complaining to Dad wouldn't help, though, any more than complaining to Michael had. Complaining to Dad had never done any good. He never heard her.

Callie took a deep breath. "Dad!" she yelled, loud enough that for a moment he was completely silent.

"Dad," she said again, more softly now, "there are some things we need to talk about."

For a moment Dad stared at her in silence.

Then he said, just as softly, "All right, Callie. But first I want you to get some sleep."

Callie heard the concern in his voice, and behind it, the love. Star wasn't the only one who cared about her.

Callie fell asleep as soon as she crawled into bed. For the first time since arriving in Tucson, she didn't dream at all.

Chapter Fifteen

In the end, some things worked out and other things didn't. Mom and Dad said they'd try to listen more and yell less; Callie said she'd do the same. No one promised anything. They just said they'd do the best they could.

What would have happened to Michael if he and his family had sat down and talked? There was no way to know. How had his family felt when he left and never came back?

Melissa offered to switch bedrooms with Callie. She grumbled as she said it, though, and Callie knew she didn't mean it. Most likely Mom and Dad had asked her to suggest the change. Callie said she'd rather stay where she was, which was true. Even though Star would probably never stand by her window again, Callie didn't want to give up her view of the yard and the mountains. Besides, her parents finally took her to a decorating store to pick out carpeting and paint.

Mom and Dad believed Callie when she said she'd run away and spent the night in the moun-

Janni Lee Simner

tains. Melissa didn't. She stared at Callie doubtfully throughout her explanation. Callie could tell that Melissa wanted to know what had really happened. Melissa didn't ask out loud, though. Callie was glad. She didn't want to tell her sister about Star, not ever.

Callie did tell someone, however. She still remembered her fight with Amy, and how upset Amy had been when she couldn't see the horse. A few days after she talked to her parents, Callie talked to Amy. As they sat on the patio with cold glasses of lemonade, Callie explained about Star, about her dreams, about the fire.

Amy was silent for a long time when Callie was through, and Callie feared her friend still didn't believe her. A pinkish-gray lizard crawled up the leg of Callie's chair, then disappeared beneath it.

Amy brushed her hair out of her face and adjusted her hat. "I'm sorry," she said quietly.

"Sorry? What for?" Callie stared at her.

"For not believing you."

Callie laughed. "I don't think I would have believed it, either, if someone else had told me."

For once, Amy didn't laugh with her. "But I should have. Because the same thing happened to me."

"You saw a horse?" Callie asked, startled.

"No. I saw my parents." Amy kicked a

133

pebble across the patio. "It was a few months after they'd died. I was in bed, almost asleep, and when I looked up I saw them standing by the doorway, watching me. I jumped out of bed and ran to them, but they disappeared before I got there. No one believed me when I tried to explain. Not even Josh. First he said I was just upset and tired. Then he said I didn't know what was real and what wasn't." Amy avoided Callie's gaze. "And then I did the same thing to you when you told me about Star."

They were silent for a while. "You didn't know," Callie finally said. "It's not your fault."

Amy smiled. "Star really does sound like a neat horse," she said. "I wish I could have seen her."

"So do I," Callie said.

"It's too bad your parents won't let you go riding."

Callie grinned. Then she told Amy about the last thing her parents had agreed to.

They'd agreed to let her take riding lessons. Not for free. Even though lessons were cheaper in Tucson than in New York, and even though Josh had agreed to teach Callie at a reasonable price, Mom and Dad weren't willing just to pay for the lessons themselves. They said they thought Callie was old enough to take on some responsibility for getting what she wanted. And they decided on a way that she could work off the cost.

Mom and Dad wanted to clean the backyard so they could landscape it. Callie agreed to help in return for her lessons.

Judging by the rusted old fences and the unruly bushes and weeds scattered about, cleaning the yard would take a long time. That was okay; Callie wanted lots of lessons. When the yard was clean, maybe Mom and Dad would let her help with the planting, too. Callie already knew how she wanted to decorate the yard: with lots of cacti and local trees, so that it held as much of the desert as possible.

Callie's first lesson was less than a week after Star had left. Josh introduced her to Pepper, a chestnut mare with white speckles. Pepper's eyes were a beautiful chocolate color, but they held nothing more than the ordinary gentleness of most horse eyes.

Josh was surprised at how easily Callie mounted, at how comfortable she looked in the saddle.

Callie took the reins in her hands, just the way Josh told her to. She reached forward and scratched Pepper's ears.

Walk, Callie thought.

Pepper just stood there, not moving. Callie sighed.

"Give her a little pressure with your legs to get her started," Josh said.

Callie squeezed. Pepper ignored her. She squeezed harder, and Pepper walked slowly around the ring. Riding normal horses was going to take a lot more work than riding Star. Callie was determined to learn, though. The world was full of normal, flesh-and-blood horses, after all.

Pepper slowed to a stop. Callie tightened her legs to start her walking again.

Out of the corner of her eye, Callie thought she saw something—a silver-gray horse, with a white mark like a star on her forehead, walking beside her.

When Callie blinked, the horse was gone. She decided she'd imagined it and kept riding.

About the Author

JANNI LEE SIMNER grew up on Long Island and has been making her way west ever since. Unlike Callie Fern, she took nearly a decade crossing the Midwest, spending much of it in St. Louis. She currently lives in Tucson, where she enjoys horseback riding and hiking in the mountains that surround the city. She has published short stories in more than a dozen anthologies, including *Starfarer's Dozen*, *Bruce Coville's Book of Nightmares*, and *Bruce Coville's Book of Magic*. *Ghost Horse* is her first novel.

Callie helped Star before... Now it's the ghost horse's turn to help her!

THE HAUNTED TRAIL

Phantom Rider

by *Janni Lee Simner*

*C*allie can't wait to go on a desert ride with her friends. But when the magical ghost horse, Star, suddenly appears, the other horses run away — leaving the entire group stranded in the desert during a torrential rainstorm! Can Callie convince an angry Star to save them from sure disaster?

Appearing soon at a bookstore near you.